RACHEL SINCLAIR
WRONGFUL CONVICTION

By Rachel Sinclair

Southern California Legal Thrillers

Presumed Guilty
Justice Delayed
Insanity Defense
Wrongful Conviction
The Trial

Vinci Books

vinci-books.com

Published by Vinci Books Ltd in 2025

1

Copyright © Rachel Sinclair 2019

The author has asserted their moral right to be identified as the author of this work in accordance with the Copyright, Designs and Patents Act 1988. This work is a work of fiction. Names, characters, places and incidents are the product of the author's imagination or are used fictitiously. Any resemblance to actual persons, living or dead, places and incidents is entirely coincidental.

All rights reserved. No part of this publication may be copied, reproduced, distributed, stored in any retrieval system, or transmitted in any form or by any means, including photocopying, recording, or other electronic or mechanical methods, nor used as a source for any form of machine learning including AI datasets, without the prior written permission of the publisher.

The publisher and the author have made every effort to obtain permissions for any third party material used in this book and to comply with copyright law. Any queries in this respect should be brought to the attention of the publisher and any omissions will be corrected in future editions.

A CIP catalogue record for this book is available from the British Library.

Paperback ISBN: 9781036702939

Printed and bound in Great Britain by Clays Ltd, Elcograf S.p.A.

Chapter One

CHRISTIAN

I JUST GOT A NEW CASE – Jamel Jackson. I felt privileged to be representing him, because I had read about his case in the paper, and I couldn't help but think that he was getting a raw deal. He had been convicted of raping an actress. Not just any actress, but an A-list actress by the name of Felicity McDaniel. I had been following the case along and I just had a feeling there was something missing in the entire procedure.

So, when I went to see him in the jail, unannounced, I talked to him to get a sense as to what happened. The kid was just 18 and had been convicted for the rape of Ms. McDaniel, and to say he was frightened would be an understatement.

"Why are you here to see me?" he asked me. He was a slight African-American boy, only about 5'6" and probably a buck thirty, with braided hair, *café au lait* skin and fine features. He had obviously been crying, as his big brown eyes were bloodshot and red. "They just put me in jail. I'm going be serving life in prison. I don't have the money to pay nobody for an appeal, if that's what you're thinking."

He looked down at his hands, which were shackled, as were his legs. I knew he was due to be transferred to the state penitentiary, in Victorville, California, within days. From the looks of him, the prospect of going to a maximum security prison was terrifying for him. As it would be for anybody in his shoes.

I had a strong feeling this was an innocent boy looking back at me, and I knew nobody was going take his case. It was not only the fact that he had no money, but also because this was a case nobody wanted to touch with a 10 foot pole. Still, his situation did not deter me. Once I had a feeling an injustice was done, that's all I really knew.

"Listen, you only need to know one thing," I said. "And that's that I'm interested in your case. I don't even expect you to pay me. I know you don't have the money."

Jamel looked at me suspiciously. "Yeah, dog, don't nobody do nothing for free. Why do I think this will cost me more than cash?"

I folded my hands in front of me and looked at him silently. I was studying him, just as he was studying me. What I didn't really want to tell him was that I was very interested in this case because I just had a feeling the person who really raped Felicity was somebody who really needed go down, and hard. There was a shadowy figure behind his entire case, and I just had a feeling it was somebody who deserved justice. I wanted to be the one to give it to him.

What I knew about this case was that there was no DNA found inside of Felicity. She, herself, had no recollection of what had happened to her - she was beaten that badly. She'd been in the hospital for several months before she was even able to talk to the cops. She had severe memory loss and her abdomen had been kicked so viciously that she was bleeding internally. These were just her internal injuries. Externally, she had been savagely kicked, so she was bruised everywhere. Her eyes were swollen shut and it took the best plastic surgeon in Los Angeles to bring her to where she looked like herself again.

The best I could tell, the reason why this poor guy was in jail, and convicted, was because he was at the wrong place at the wrong time. He had explained to the court that he was an Uber delivery driver and Felicity apparently had ordered a sub sandwich from Subway to have delivered to her house. However, by the time he got there, according to what his court testimony was, he'd found she was not answering the door. He didn't know what to do, because he was new on the job, and didn't realize that in cases where the person doesn't answer the door, you're supposed to indicate on the app that nobody was answering, and then you have to wait a certain amount of time. If the person doesn't answer the phone or the door within that window of time, you can leave the food at the door and take a picture of it.

However, as Jamel had explained in his testimony, he wasn't aware of that provision. He thought he had to make every effort to deliver the food. So he'd gone around to the pool area to see if he could find her, and, he told the court, he found her laying by the pool, unconscious. He called 911 and they came to take her to the hospital. She almost died.

Of course, the prosecutor made hay about the fact that he was able to get into the pool area in the first place. After all, the pool area of her house was locked with a combination lock. The assumption was that if he was telling the truth, and he really was an Uber driver, and he just wanted to deliver her food, come hell or high water, he would not have been able to get back there.

This was one of the first errors I found in the case. His defense attorney did a terrible job. I knew that I would have to comb the transcripts for any kind of error the court made, but I knew that in the end, I would probably have to go with an ineffective assistance of counsel defense and try for a writ of *habeas corpus*. His defense attorney never even proposed the question of how would Jamel have been able to get back into the pool area even if he was the rapist. If the pool area was locked, it was locked. In fact, that was the entire hole in the entire case as far as I was concerned – there was no reasonable explanation as to how he could've gotten on the grounds in the first place. To me, the entire thing seemed to be a huge set-up.

I wasn't sure, but my instinct told me that what had happened was that the actual person who beat and raped her did so and then summoned an Uber delivery driver to come and deliver food, with the intention of eventually setting up the driver, whoever it was. The person who raped her deliberately left the pool area open and left the gate to her home open, and that person had taken the chance that the Uber driver would not have known that you're not supposed to go onto private property to deliver food. Indeed, I had reviewed the rules for Uber delivery drivers, and that's one of the things that they're not supposed to do – they are not supposed to go onto private property. If the person doesn't answer the door, the person doesn't answer the door. You leave the food at the door and go.

So the prosecutor was able to make hay about that entire thing as well. He was able to show that since it was Uber policy not to go onto private property, that meant Jamel's protestations that he was an innocent bystander were bullshit, because if he really was just an innocent

Uber driver, he would've followed the policy like he was supposed to.

Of course, if the defense attorney was doing his job, he would've hammered home the fact that Jamel was, indeed, delivering Uber at the time Felicity was found. That would have been easy enough to prove - all he would have to have done was subpoena the Uber dispatch to show that Jamel had indeed taken an order to Felicity's house and delivered it at that time. That would have bolstered Jamel's story. But the defense attorney didn't even bother to do that, so the prosecutor was able to successfully make the argument to the jury that Jamel wasn't delivering at that time, but that he had wandered in off the street, was able to scale the wall to Felicity's mansion and then scale the wall to her pool area, where he raped and beat her and then called 911.

None of it made sense to me. I knew Felicity's walls around her house and around her pool were made of stone and were 10 feet tall. The prosecutor was not able to really establish that Jamel would've been able to scale either one of those walls, let alone both of them, but again, the defense attorney did not question the theory that Jamel got onto the grounds by scaling the walls. In fact, the defense attorney did not even bother to go to the site and see exactly how high these walls really were.

There were so many errors committed by his attorney that I couldn't even count them all. Unfortunately, I had a harder time trying to find errors the court had made. It seemed to me that the court really didn't make too many errors in the case, but the defense attorney was another story. He made a ton.

And, at this point, I was cynical. I had seen what happened when people were corrupted by the system, and I knew there was a good chance the defense attorney might've been paid off to throw the case. Of course, I had no proof of that, but I did know that he was extraordinarily incompetent. I also knew that *somebody* would be convicted of raping this poor woman. An A-list actress was raped, beaten so badly that she was practically in a coma, she lost her memory, and she had to have extensive plastic surgeries to return her to normal. Somebody would pay for that. So, after reading through the facts of the case, and the transcripts, I realized that what happened was that somebody would pay for doing that to her, and Jamel was unfortunately the closest person the prosecutor could find to pin the blame on.

The reason why I was convinced the true culprit was somebody well-connected was just the fact that so many things had gone wrong in this case. It wasn't *just* that the defense attorney did not object to things that were clearly objectionable, and there were quite a few things that were objectionable, and it wasn't *just* the fact that the defense attorney failed to put on exculpatory evidence, such as showing the walls of the compound were way too tall for a small boy like Jamel to have scaled. It was everything about this case. It stunk to high heaven.

"Jamel, here's the thing," I said to him. "At this point, I don't think you really have a choice but to trust me. What do you have to lose? You just told me you don't have the money to hire somebody to file an appeal for you, so, as I see it, it's either me or nobody. You're already convicted of raping Felicity McDaniel. You have a chance to actually get out of your prison sentence, and that chance lies with one person – me."

He shook his head. "No, don't get me wrong. I know what you're saying, and I know that if somebody don't help me, I'm going to spend the rest of my life in prison for something I had nothing to do with. But I just don't know what's in it for you."

I took a deep breath. "Listen, here's the thing. I went to law school because I knew far too many of my friends who were going into the joint for nonviolent drug offenses. That's how they cleaned up my neighborhood – cops would sweep anybody and everybody who was caught with so much as a joint and make sure they got the book thrown at them. Of course, the only people who were subjected to this kind of treatment were minorities – the black and brown people. On the other hand, I could stand on the street corner and smoke a joint and cops would drive by me and look the other way. But if there was a black boy, or a Hispanic boy, or girl for that matter, they couldn't do anything on the street. If they had so much as a dime bag on their person, they were harassed, and, trust me, the cops harassed people on my street and they would be charged with intent to distribute and be put away for a long time. So after seeing one person after another on my street go to prison for what should have been a misdemeanor possession, I decided to do something about it. The thing that I decided to do was to go to law school so that I could help people like the people I grew up with."

At this, Jamel smiled. "Come on, you're putting me on. You're not from the streets."

"Why do you say that?"

"Look at you. You got lots of money, I can tell." He was looking at my Rolex watch and he nodded approvingly. "That watch costs more than what my mama makes in an entire year. Twice as much as what she makes. I can just tell it's not hot. I mean, you get these clowns in the hood selling that shit on the street, but you know it's made in Taiwan and it's going to break by the end of the day. But I can tell that that's the real shit right there. No, you ain't never been on the streets. But that's all right. I'm sure you have your reasoning for trying to get me out of this place. I think you probably just want the publicity, but, as my mama says, I'm not going to look no gift horse in the mouth."

I was telling him the truth about my neighborhood. It was a rough place to grow up, especially if you're a minority. But I knew I presented as a rich guy and I wasn't going to convince this kid otherwise, so I let it go.

"That's good. Listen, here's what I'm going to do. I'm going to take your case and file a notice of appeal immediately. I think we have a very good chance of getting your conviction overturned, but in the meantime, I really want to prove your actual innocence. I know there was no DNA found on Felicity, so it's going to be difficult to try to prove your innocence, but I'm going to try to do just that. At any rate, even if I can't show the appellate court that you're actually innocent, I want to make the case for your new trial. And I can almost assure you that you'll get a new trial."

I took a deep breath, hoping I wasn't promising too much. It wasn't like me to make a claim like I just made to him – that I could for sure get him off his charge. But, at the same time, I knew there was a good chance that would happen.

Jamel was looking at me now, his eyes scrunched up and with a look on his face like he just could not understand anything about what was going on. "Listen, I'm okay with walking this prison sentence down. I got a brother in the system, half-brother really, and he tells me things aren't so bad behind bars. To tell the truth, I was having a hard time trying to make ends meet on the streets. I mean, I was driving Uber and all that shit, but they don't pay nothing.

And you know that most of the money that I was making through Uber was going into the tank. I ain't got a pot to piss in and that's the truth. Listen, I know kids like me, we don't get a lot of breaks in this world. We certainly don't get to have defense attorneys just take our cases for free. I still don't know what your game is, but you're right about one thing – you are the only game in town for me. So, I'll let you represent me."

I took a deep breath. My home base was in San Diego, of course, and this kid was convicted in Los Angeles County. But he was being taken to the Victorville prison, and that would've been the same thing if he would have been convicted in San Diego County, so I figured that it wouldn't be too much of a burden to represent him.

I left him with a handshake and an assurance that I would be working on his case as soon as possible.

I called Avery in my car on the way home.

"I saw Jamel and he's going to be my new client."

"Are you sure about this?" Avery was concerned about my taking on this case because she knew it would be hard on me if I lost. She also knew that it would be hard on me to travel, because the District Court of Appeals was here in Los Angeles County. But, at the same time, I knew I didn't have to really make too many appearances in court, so it really wasn't that big of a deal for me.

What would be somewhat hard on me was the fact that I was determined to find the real person who had raped this woman, which meant I would have to make a lot of trips up to Los Angeles to try to figure that one out. I would have to talk to a lot of people, and I would have to make more than one pilgrimage to the actual site where she was raped. But, for the time being, it was just a matter of me getting back to my office in San Diego and combing through the transcripts for all the errors, and then doing my research, writing out a brief, and scheduling an oral argument as soon as possible.

"I'm serious as a heart attack about this. Listen, this kid has no money and if I don't represent him, he's going to have to represent himself. Or find a jailhouse lawyer and we know how good they are." Truth be told, I knew quite a few people who were good jailhouse lawyers, but at the same time, they weren't exactly lawyers. They were just inmates who knew their way around the prison research libraries, and other inmates hired them to try to write out their appeals. That's how most inmates actually did their appeals, because there is not a right to an appellate counsel under the Constitution, so, once you're convicted, and you're poor, it's very difficult to find somebody to take your case, because you're not eligible for the public defender's office anymore.

"Okay, just remember you have a full roster of other cases right here in San Diego County, so you can't put too much time into this case. But if you feel strongly this kid is innocent and he didn't get a break, then, by all means, go for it."

I knew Avery would be all for my taking this case because of her background of being wrongfully convicted herself. It turned out that, in her case, the person who actually murdered her friend was a rich bastard by the name of Carl. He was running a sex trafficking ring, one that was well attended by very well-heeled people, and he had plenty of protection.

Why did I think it would be a similar case here?

Chapter Two

JAMEL

JAMEL WENT BACK to his cell after he saw the white guy who would try to actually see if he could get him out of prison. He knew he was about to be transferred to Victorville, and, as far as he knew, white guy or no, he would spend the rest of his life behind bars. That was just something he had come to terms with long ago.

Oh, he was grateful somebody had taken an interest in him. He just didn't think anything would come of it. He knew the score. He was a black kid, disposable. In fact, he wasn't just disposable, but a lot of people actively hated him just for the color of his skin. He knew that, within the past few years, the racism that had always been bubbling beneath the surface of this country had started boiling over. Suddenly, he was being attacked with racial slurs, almost daily, and people were always calling the cops on him for the slightest things. Such as the time he was in the park just laying in the grass. He had a blanket underneath him and was just enjoying the day. Some guy called the cops on him, apparently telling the cops that he was a homeless guy in the park and had to be dealt with. The cops came out and questioned him. He had to show the cops that he did actually have a home. In fact, the cops escorted him there. If he didn't have a home, he thought he probably would've spent the night in jail as a vagrant.

Another time, he was going into his apartment but had forgotten his key-card. This was when he actually had a full-time job, working construction, so he could afford a place of his own. He had since lost that job, due to budget cut-backs, and had been driving Uber ever since. On the day he forgot his key-card, he waited until somebody else entered the building and then went in with him. As he walked into the building, a white lady questioned him. She said she hadn't seen him around before, and she saw he didn't have a key card, so what was he doing there? He tried to show her that he had a key to his own apartment, but that didn't satisfy her. She also called the cops, who came out to question him, and, once again, he had to prove to the cops that he had an apartment in that building.

He knew that if he didn't have black skin that there was no way anyone would ever call the cops on him for simply relaxing in the park or getting into his own building, but he also knew that lots of his friends were also having the cops called on them for no real reason. Living while black was a crime anymore, and he knew that had gotten worse over the years and was just going to get worse and worse.

So, when he was arrested for raping this woman, even though he was the one who called 911, and if it weren't for him, she probably would've died, he knew he would get convicted for it. It was a foregone conclusion in his mind. This lady was raped, there was nobody else who would have the crime pinned on them, he was in the wrong place at the wrong time, and none of that mattered. What mattered was that he couldn't afford to hire an attorney, so he was assigned one, and the attorney he was assigned could not have cared less about his case. In fact, Jamel had the distinct impression that his attorney just wanted to get it over with, mainly because the case had attracted so much publicity, and his attorney, Jim Stack, didn't like the glare. Which was a reason why, when it came time to ask him to put on evidence on his behalf, Jim told the court he would rest. That meant he didn't call any witnesses and did not put on any kind of evidence on his behalf.

What was so sad was that Jamel just kind of shrugged his shoulders about his attorney's laziness and incompetence. He figured that was what he deserved, in a society like this that was not colorblind in any way, shape or form. He figured that it was just another way for a kid like him to get off the streets, not that he was ever on the streets, because, after all, he did have a job. Yes, it was a job driving Uber, so it didn't pay a whole lot. He was now living in a rented room that he found for only $500 a month, a tiny room in an old dilapidated house on the east side of Los Angeles, but, nevertheless, it was a home. His home. So, even though he knew the jury looked at him like he was a street kid, he really wasn't. He didn't deal drugs. He didn't gang bang. His mama had taught him right from wrong and kept him away from all that.

Yet, there he was, in jail awaiting transfer to the big house.

The tragedy was that he didn't even think it was necessarily unfair. It was what it was.

So even though this white boy, this Christian Davis boy,

wanted to work his case, he didn't think it would come to anything. He just figured Christian would try to get him a new trial, but there was nothing that could be done for a guy like him.

Still, he was happy that Christian was even going to try.

Chapter Three

THE MAN

THE MAN KNEW he had a problem. He always had known that. He had been protected for most of his life by his father, and then, when he got to be in his 40s, and his father no longer wanted to protect him, he was still protected by plenty of other people. He started to believe in his mind that he was above the law. After all, it wasn't like he had ever been arrested for anything he had ever done in his life. And he knew that he had done plenty in his life, things that should have landed him prison for life, but they did not.

For instance, when he was 17 years old, he raped his first woman. He had started to understand from an even earlier age that there was no way he could ever attain any kind of sexual satisfaction unless there was violence involved. He beat up his first prostitute at the age of 13, and, even at that time, he was built like a brick shithouse, so he was able to overpower the woman who had been hired as a prostitute for him by his own father. She was a slight woman, only 5'2" and a hundred pounds or so, weak as a kitten. At that time, he was 6'3" and 200 pounds of sheer muscle. Now, he was 6'6" and 225 pounds of sheer muscle, so he was able to overpower just about anybody.

That woman, he didn't know her name then, let alone trying to know it now - she was just a whore - he had beat senseless to a pulp. He had savagely pummeled her with his fists, pulled her hair, kicked her, and she let him do it. It wasn't until he had actually finished with what he did to her that he found out why she let him do it – apparently his father had paid her extra to participate in S and M games. She was paid an extra thousand dollars, so she knew she would get beaten up and so she just took it.

That infuriated him. He hated masochists. He never wanted to be with anybody who took pleasure in the beatings he would give to them. If a person was taking pleasure in what he was doing to them, then it took away his pleasure, and that's all he really knew. So when he found out his father had paid this whore an extra thousand dollars for the beating he gave her, he knew he would have to find his own whores, and not pay them anything extra, and just beat them savagely. And it was important to him that they screamed and begged for mercy.

So, for several years, that was what he did – he got his jollies by picking up people, paid for by his father, because he was a minor who didn't have money of his own, and beating them. He didn't have sex with any of them, but he did beat them.

Then, when he was 17 years old, and he finally was not a virgin anymore, he decided to rape women, as many women as he possibly could. He didn't even care. He didn't discriminate with his whores. They were young, old, and everything in between. Black, white, Hispanic, Asian, he never really cared. He was always very careful all of his life, however, to make sure he found people who were marginalized in some way. Homeless people, prostitutes, people who had zero power. The reason why he did that was because he knew that people like that were disposable and nobody really cared if they were raped, murdered or beaten up.

That was how he got away with savagely raping and beating women in his younger years. In one of the few times he slipped up and actually found a victim who was not marginalized – such as a college girl he raped on the UCLA campus, who turned out to have a father who was a physician at Sharp Hospital in LA – he had to make sure his father paid everybody off to make sure he did not stand trial for what he did to her.

After he raped the girl, her name was, oh he forgot her name, his father took him aside and warned him not to do that again.

"Listen, I don't really care what you do, but you have to do it to people who don't matter. You have to stay with the prostitutes, the vagrants, poor people on the streets. When you go around raping pretty little white girls on campus, your butt's going to be in a sling next time, because I won't be able to protect you."

He could say nothing to his father. He could never say anything to his father. His father beat on him savagely from the time he was only five years old. His father would beat on him for the most minor of things, so the man knew his father would possibly kill him if he didn't do as he was told. His father terrified him. He was like a little boy around him.

So, from that point on, he did as his father had told him – he stuck to only preying on people who did not have the means to fight back. The people who society did not care about. And that was fine with him - he just needed to make sure he got his sexual aggression out on somebody. He didn't really care who they were.

Of course, Felicity was a different story.

If it weren't for the fact that he had such a good plan in place for someone to take the fall, he knew he would be in prison right that very second.

He made a mistake in doing what he did to her, but she had it coming.

That's all he really knew.

Chapter Four

CHRISTIAN

THE FIRST THING I did when I got to the office was prepare a notice of appeal. That was the first step I had to take, and then, of course, the next step would be to throw myself into writing an appellate brief.

I went and saw Avery, because I knew I would need help with preparing this brief. I was not exactly the best researcher in the entire world, although I did have mad writing skills. So I knew I could make this brief the best I could possibly make it.

When I got to Avery's office, she looked up at me.

"Hey, Christian, what's going on?" she asked.

"I'm going to need a researcher for my brief. You got anybody in mind?"

"No, but there are always kids from law school who want to get some experience in. You should look there first. What about the transcript? You see anything that stands out to you as far as errors made by the court?"

"Not so much errors made by the court, but I definitely have a really good leg to stand on as far as ineffective assistance of counsel. There's lots of evidence about that. So I think my best bet would be to file a writ of *habeas corpus*, and, if that doesn't work out, I'll try a regular appeal, although that does not look as good."

"I wouldn't know a thing about that, would I?" she said with a roll of her eyes.

I knew what Avery with thinking. She was the expert as far as ineffective assistance of counsel arguments went. Of course, Avery's counsel in her criminal case was ineffective because she was paid to be that way. Avery served 7 years in prison for killing her best childhood friend. She found out who really did it – it was a rich bastard, of course – and she found out her attorney in that case took a bribe to throw it.

I wondered if the same thing was going on here. I would not be surprised.

Then again, this case, in general, was the kind of thing that was faced by poor defendants. Poor people didn't get the best representation because they couldn't afford it. They had to go with court-appointed attorneys who were often overwhelmed and underpaid. Even in death penalty cases in many states, the attorneys were under-compensated and were often inexperienced. For instance, some states paid only $1,000 to try a death penalty cases. There would be no way the attorney could do any investigation or hire any experts for that kind of money. Even when a client had to go with the public defender's offices, which was mostly the case with poor defendants like Jamel, the offices and the attorneys were underfunded. One attorney might be dealing with a hundred felony cases at any one time while getting paid $40,000 a year. They were doing God's work, as far as I was concerned, fighting the good fight and doing what they could, but when you're that overwhelmed, mistakes will be made.

No doubt about it, I knew that in this country that if you didn't have money, you were nobody in the criminal justice system. That's why so many black and brown people ended up in prison for minor crimes. That's why so many black and brown people ended up in prison for things nobody else would go to prison for. It was the reason why rich people basically stayed out of prison, no matter what they did. I was still shocked they were able to bring down big fish from time to time, such as Martha Stewart and Bernie Madoff but, mainly, if you had a lot of money and connections, you were above the law. Look at Jeffrey Epstein, who raped young girls for years. He finally was arrested for what he did, although look how long that took. Look at the sweetheart deal he got in Florida, just because he had a lot of money and a lot of connections. He was raping young girls and essentially got sentenced to house arrest and had to go to jail for an hour a day. The rest of the time he was at his beach house in Florida. Of course, that all came to an end when he finally was arrested for real and facing real time, and then killed himself in prison. So, justice finally came for him, but look how long it took - years and years.

I was determined that Jamel wouldn't be just another statistic. He wouldn't be just another black boy who went to prison for something he had nothing to do with. If it was the last thing I did in this life, I would make sure of it. I knew there were millions of other kids who looked just like him, kids being harassed on the street and put into prison for non-violent crimes or crimes that they had nothing to do with, like Jamel. Some of these innocent people were on death row. I could not save them all. But I would save this one, and maybe that could earn me some modicum of peace in life.

I would not only have to get a law student to do the research for me, but I would also have to get Regina on the case to see if she could find out who really did this.

So, I called her. "Hey, Regina, it's Christian."

She chuckled a little. "Hey, Christian, I hear you got a good appellate case. What can I do you for?"

"I need you to find out who really did it. With any luck, I'm going to be able to get a new trial for this kid, and then if I do get a new trial for him, obviously I want to hit the ground running. If we can find out who really raped this woman, we can go a long way towards showing the jury that Jamel should've never been in prison in the first place."

"OK, where do you want me to begin?"

"I hate to do this to you, but you're probably going to have to go to her house in Los Angeles and take a look around. I'll get an order from the judge to allow you to do that. You're also going to have to talk to the people she knew."

"I guess I can probably try to straighten it all out. Just give me a few days, I'll try to get a few leads. In the meantime, what are the chances you'll be able to get an appellate court to overturn the verdict?"

"I'd say it's probably about even. In reading the transcript, I can tell you there were a lot of mistakes the defense attorney made. A lot of them. That's going to be the only way I can get this guy off, I think."

"Good luck."

"Thanks. Hey, what's going on with you and Aidan?"

Regina had finally decided to give Aidan a chance. I felt so badly for him because he had been mooning over her for so long. Everybody knew he had been, not that he knew that everybody knew. As far as Aidan was concerned, nobody knew about the way he felt about her. Of course that was bullshit. Obviously, he was infatuated with her. But she never wanted to give him the time of day, mainly because of her background. She hadn't had good luck with men in her past, to say the very least.

"Hey, I don't talk about that. But, I will say we're hanging out and that's as far as it's going to go for right now. " And then she paused. "We're dating, OK? Is that what you wanted to know? Not that that's any of your business."

I had to have a laugh. She was so defensive but she was more defensive about this subject than any other subject that I could ever ask her about. I knew why, of course. She didn't like people prying into her personal life.

"I don't really care, I was just curious. I know he's always had a thing for you and I just wanted to know if that thing got off the ground yet."

"It did. And that's all you need to know. So listen, give me a few days and I'll try to figure out what happened in this case."

"Thanks."

I DECIDED to see what I could do as far as connecting with somebody who could do legal research for me. So, I put a word in with the University of San Diego, which had the largest law school in the area, and I also put in a word with UCLA. Obviously, UCLA had a much bigger law school than the University of San Diego did and were more likely to have stellar students willing to do research on this case for not too much money.

Just then, I looked at the clock and realized I was late for a hearing. I was perpetually running late because I was always going from one hearing to another. I didn't have too many trials under my belt yet, mainly because most cases don't go to trial. I had quite a few people who I was pleading out, because I had to face facts – most people I represented were good for their crimes. I knew the people I represented were the ones getting arrested for crimes other people would not be arrested for. But it was what it was.

Chapter Five

JAMEL

JAMEL WAS TRANSFERRED to Victorville the day after he saw his new attorney. He was on the bus with the other guys going to prison and he felt a sense of fear, maybe for the first time. Although he had come to terms with the fact that he would be spending the rest of his life behind bars, somehow the reality of being on the bus on the way to this place filled him with apprehension.

He didn't know what to expect, although he kind of did. His half-brother told him what to expect and told him he would have to get protection behind bars. It would be the first thing he would have to do. He was already somewhat famous because the case of Felicity and her being raped was something in the news quite a bit over the course of the months that the trial went on. So he knew he would be well-known, but that didn't really ease his fears that much.

His mama had come to see him before he was put on the transfer bus and she was crying. He was her only child. His half-brother had a different mother but the same father. Jamel was regretting the fact that he would go prison just because he didn't want to let her down. It really wasn't that fair once he thought about it. He tried all of his life to keep his nose clean. It was something he prided himself on. When everybody else around him was gang-banging, drug dealing and doing things like that in the neighborhood, he didn't get into any of that. He didn't get good grades in school and he knew he couldn't go to college but he did have a strong interest in cars. It was his dream to become an auto mechanic. Which was not an easy thing to do, considering the new cars were so high-tech and computer-based. But now he was never going to get a chance to do that. He was never going to get a chance to do anything except look at the four walls of his prison cell, eat crappy food and try to stay out of trouble. That was the most important thing, his mama told him - he needed to try to keep his nose clean, even in prison. That wasn't going to be easy to do. But, according to his half-brother, Nathan, he would be able to maybe survive if he joined one of the prison gangs.

The guy who sat next to him on the bus was a white guy by the name of Charles Wyatt. He was covered in tattoos - both of his arms were, as was his chest. He had dark hair and very pale skin. He looked out the window as the bus bumped along and then finally engaged Jamel in conversation.

"You know, I thought I recognized you. You're the guy who got convicted for raping that actress, aren't you?"

Jamel felt embarrassed, as he always did. Still, he wondered what this guy did. "Yeah, that's me. I mean, it wasn't me. I had nothing to do with it, I just got convicted for it. What did you do?"

He shrugged. "Hey, I'm innocent too. We're all innocent here, aren't we?" And then he smiled. "I popped a dude. He deserved it. I was on the highway and he cut me off. So I chased him down, ran him off the road and shot him. I'm good for it. All day long."

For some reason, this guy scared the crap out of Jamel. The way he talked about killing a guy so nonchalantly, Jamel wondered if a guy like Charles would kill him for something minor as well.

Jamel didn't talk to Charles anymore on the way to the prison. He didn't want to set this guy off, and he knew he might possibly do something wrong that would do just that. He thought about his mama, crying, and how she was so devastated that her one and only child was going to prison. If there was any chance at all that he could make it out, he would do it, which meant he needed to steer clear of cold-blooded killers like this Charles.

He would make it out for her.

Chapter Six

CHRISTIAN

I FOUND a law student within a couple of days. I knew I would probably have to rent an office up in Los Angeles at least temporarily, because I was starting to understand that there might be more court appearances than I had anticipated and I also realized that most investigation would take place up in LA. It wasn't that big of a deal to make a trip up to Los Angeles once or twice a week - I could work it all around my schedule pretty easily.

The law student was named Sandy Granger. She was a third-year and explained to me that she was looking for a part-time job and was not exactly top of her class, so she was really looking for the experience. "Also, I think this is a just cause. I've followed this case as well and I really think that guy got screwed."

"Everybody thinks that," I said. "That's why I think we have a good chance of getting his conviction overturned."

"I hope you're right," Sandy said.

"Me too, me too. So, listen, I need you to comb through the transcripts. That's what I've been doing as well. I also need you to highlight for me any areas you think might have been an error. I really am looking for something the court did wrong as well, because, from the research I've done, I think it's more likely the conviction will be overturned if the court did something wrong. Unfortunately, so far, I haven't really found anything. But maybe you could."

"I'll do what I can."

I looked around the temporary office I rented in Los Angeles. I chose something facing the beach. I really missed the beach. At the moment, I was living in a condo in downtown San Diego. It was facing the water, but it faced the bay, not the Pacific Ocean. I didn't get to the ocean as often as I liked, even though Avery lived in Coronado and her condo was facing the sand. Avery was always telling me that I really didn't want to live close to the water, because everything rusted out so quickly – cars, anything metal, cookware. Still, there was something about the water that called to me, so I knew that when I got a temporary office in Los Angeles, I wanted it by the ocean.

As usual, when I took a break from all the research I was doing, I looked up and thought about Avery. I felt a little like Aidan, loving Regina from afar for so long. I felt the same way about Avery that Aidan felt about Regina. I felt the same way about her since the beginning. Of course, I never did anything about it. My office was two doors down from hers and she was always busy with her cases and I was always busy with mine. We were friends and we hung out. But that was about the extent of it.

There were other girls in the office who were dying for me to take them out, but I had no interest in them. I loved that Avery was a social justice warrior, just like me. That was why she got involved with the Esme Gutierrez case, the case that brought us together. Esme Gutierrez was an immigrant from El Salvador framed for the murder of a rich girl she lived with. Boy, did that case take a turn, as it turned out the girl who was murdered was not actually the person who everybody thought she was, but, rather, was an imposter. The real daughter had been killed years before. Avery was able to figure all that out and I was impressed with her. Impressed as hell. She was also able to figure out that the father was somebody who was not a good guy.

What impressed me the most was that she took that case for free, like I was taking this case for free. She did that because she believed in it. Of course, she had the money to do something like that, because she had been wrongfully convicted herself and won a $10 million judgment from the state of Missouri. Because of that, she had the ability to take cases she was passionate about, whether or not the defendant had any money to pay her. I loved that she did that – she was using her money as a force for good. I didn't have the same amount of money in my account, so I was less able to take cases *pro bono*, but I was comfortable enough that I knew I could take a case for free from time to time. After all, before I came to work with Avery, I was working for a big firm, making $200,000 a year. I socked away much of that money, so I wasn't hurting for cash. That enabled me to have some latitude of freedom in taking a case, like Jamel's, that I really believed in.

Chapter Seven

CHRISTIAN

I DECIDED to see Jamel's mother. I knew she would probably have some information for me and maybe I could glean something from what she told me that could help me figure out exactly what happened.

Jamel's mother lived in east Los Angeles, the neighborhood where I grew up in. I knew the environment he lived in because I lived in that same environment. It was a place of desperation, where people didn't work, couldn't find a job, and a lot of people were on welfare. But not everybody - I knew there were plenty of people working jobs for a very low wage. They were housekeepers in motels, cashiers at Walmart and fast food workers.

Sometimes, several immigrant families lived in one unit.

Jamel's mother was named Aisha Jackson. I talked to her over the phone and I could tell by the tone of her voice that she was suffering. She couldn't speak to me about Jamel without breaking down, she explained to me over the phone.

I didn't really know exactly why I wanted to see her so

badly, except that I wanted to maybe give her just a little bit of hope.

Just a tiny sliver of hope.

The apartment where she lived was extremely run down and part of a four-plex. Actually, it was a converted apartment in a large rambling home built around the turn-of-the-century. This home had been converted into four different apartments, each of them extremely small, I would imagine. The front yard was bounded by a fence, and the weeds in the front yard were 5 feet tall, easily. On the stoop of the house was a baldheaded man with a paunchy spare tire. He was drinking beer. He eyed me warily as I walked by. He was pale, white-haired and looked like he had lost all of his teeth.

"Who you coming to see?" he asked me while he gulped his beer.

"Aisha Jackson."

He nodded. He finished off his beer and then opened up another one. It was 11 o'clock in the morning. I wondered if that was all he had to do all day.

I had a feeling that's exactly what he did all day.

"She knows you're coming?" he asked me.

"Yes, she does."

"That's good. Aisha, she ain't seeing nobody. She rarely comes out of the house anymore. Well, except to go to her two jobs. Then again, maybe she won't have to work two jobs anymore, now that..." He took another drink of his beer and then looked away. The unfinished sentence was hanging in the air, but I knew what he was getting at. Now that her son was incarcerated, and she was no longer supporting him, maybe she could start working only one job.

I knew the two jobs were keeping her busy, to say the

very least. She worked 30 hours a week as a Walmart cashier and 30 hours a week working as a fry cook at a local Denny's. I felt privileged that she could take the time out to talk with me, considering her schedule was so tight.

I walked up the steps and knocked on her door.

She opened up the door and I was struck by how young she looked. Jamel was 18 years old and this woman looked like she was in her early 30s, maybe mid 30s. She was about 5'5", slender, but not skinny, with broad shoulders, small breasts, and large hips. Her hair was worn in a natural state - it was curly and held back by a red headband. She wasn't wearing any makeup, but she seemed to glow from within.

All the same, I could see an enormous amount of pain in her eyes. She probably was experiencing more pain than anybody should have to. I couldn't imagine having my only child being incarcerated. Yet I knew it was a common story for the people in this neighborhood. I knew that, because I lived it. I lived through so many people having so many of their sons taken away and their daughters too, but mainly their sons. This neighborhood, like my own neighborhood, felt like a ghost town, in a way. It was haunted by the spirits of so many young boys incarcerated in a box, never to come out again. The ones who were "lucky" enough to be released were released as a shell of their former selves. Like a war veteran, these young men had seen too much, had been subjected to too many tragedies. Their lives had been filled with pain, both before they went to prison and after, and there was just no way they could ever live a normal life.

They were too broken.

Aisha nodded. She stepped into her little tiny apartment and I followed her in. Although the carpet was threadbare and had seen better days, the place was not too bad. It was tiny - she did not even have a dining room, just a living room and a galley kitchen. The furniture was well-maintained, although it did not match – she had a leather loveseat and a floral couch. There were houseplants on various shelves. African violets, rhododendrons, that sort of thing. She seemed to have a green thumb, for they were thriving. In the corner of the apartment sang a parakeet, blue with a white head. An enormous black and white cat came up to greet me when I walked in the door. It immediately went to a scratching post before leaping on a kitty tower.

I could tell Aisha had been crying. Her eyes were red and bloodshot, and, on her coffee table, right in front of the loveseat, was a box of Kleenex. Around the box of Kleenex were some wads of used tissues. She discreetly picked them up and threw them in the trash.

"Um," she said to me and then started to cry. She motioned to the loveseat, and I sat down, understanding what she was trying to get at. She nodded when I sat down on the love-seat and then she sat down on the couch, which was cater-corner to the loveseat, and sat back.

"I'm so sorry, I'm really not that bad of a hostess usually, but –" she started to cry again. "Can I get you anything to drink? Water, anything?"

I shook my head. I didn't want her to get up and try to entertain me. I mainly just wanted to be there to try to reassure her that there was a possibility her son would be getting out, hopefully soon.

"No, really, that's okay. I'm really sorry to be barging in on you like this," I said.

She shook her head. "Oh, no. Please don't say that. You're taking my son's case and not asking any money for it. I feel like God sent you to Jamel and to me. I've been praying on this every single night, ever since he was arrested. I've been praying on this and praying on this. You wouldn't believe how much I've been praying. And here you are." She got another Kleenex, dabbed her eyes, and blew her nose. "I couldn't believe he was convicted. I just couldn't believe it. My son is a good boy. A good boy. I know he would never do anything like this. But the jury convicted him. I don't understand. My son is not a violent boy. Never been violent. Never shown any connection to violence. He's always been very helpful to me around the house. He's always been my shining light. You know, I never had the easiest time in life. I had him when I was only 15 years old." She took a deep breath. "He came about because of a rape. I was walking home from the bus when a stranger pushed me into the bushes and did it to me. I was a virgin. I didn't press charges against the person, because I didn't know who he was. He was a masked man. There was no way I could've ever identified him. I guess I was lucky he was masked, because maybe if he wasn't, I could have identified him so he would've killed me. And I've been laying awake nights, wondering, that…" She shook her head and took a deep breath. "I'm afraid. I'm afraid maybe Jamel did this. Maybe he has his father's genes and was born violent. I don't want to ever believe that. I don't want to think that way. I know I've raised him with the best values I could. I've done the best I could, being all alone like this. But what if I didn't do enough? What if…" She shook her head. "What if he never had a chance?" Her voice was a hoarse whisper at this point. "I mean, I never even thought about having an abortion. Even though I was raped and pregnant because of the rape, I've never even thought about killing my child. Now I kind of wonder if maybe I should have. Did I raise a monster? I thought he was a good boy, but what if he wasn't? I have these questions every single day."

I reached over to her hand, putting my hand on top of hers. "Listen, I don't pretend to be able to answer those questions for you. I can tell you that I feel your son has a chance to get out of prison. I saw enough mistakes in the transcript that I think that if I do a stellar job with this appellate case, he has a good chance to walk free. If I can get his conviction overturned, he might get another trial. I'm also trying to find the person who really did this so Jamel has a chance to be acquitted in another trial. If he has another trial, I'll be his attorney and I won't make the same kind of mistakes his other attorney did."

"I don't believe you," Aisha said. "I'm so sorry. I don't want to tell you that. But I talked to some friends of mine. They have sons that are also imprisoned. They all told me they've been trying to get their sons out of prison and they can't. They have never actually had an appeal because they can't afford a lawyer, but their sons have tried to write their own appeals behind bars. Nobody has the money for legal representation around these parts. When Jamel told me you're taking his case for free, I just couldn't believe it. I just hope you're not wasting your time. You seem like such a nice man."

"I *am* a nice man. But, more than that, I really believe in your son's case. And, to be honest with you, it just didn't make sense to me. It didn't make sense that a kid like that could scale such high walls to get to this Felicity person."

She nodded. "I know. That didn't make sense to me either and I was sitting there at the trial the whole time. I missed a lot of work to attend his trial because the trial went on for weeks. Weeks I had to take off work and did not get paid. I was about to be evicted from my apartment and I lost my car. I have to ride the bus everywhere now, but it was worth it to make sure my son knew I was right behind him the entire way. But you're right, nothing in this case made sense to me either."

I looked at her and saw in her face that she was starting to feel the essence of hope. Her eyes were brighter than when I first met her – when she answered the door, there wasn't a light behind her brown eyes. Now, I saw that light, although it was only a flicker. Her posture was just a tad bit straighter. She looked me in the eye, whereas, when she first answered the door to let me in, she was looking down at my shoes.

I could not let this woman down.

I swallowed hard. "Ms. Jackson," I began.

She waved her hand at me dismissively. "Aisha, please," she said with a big smile on her face. Her smile was genuine and beautiful – her teeth were perfectly straight and her entire face lit up when she smiled.

"Aisha, I really don't want you to think this is a slam-dunk. It's anything but. Very few cases get overturned – only about 12% of all cases on appeal are reversed in some way. It's going to be a long road. Even if the appellate court reverses, it will probably remand it back to the trial court, which means the trial court will get another crack at the case. That means the entire thing will start all over again, with the same witnesses, the same judge and all of that. A different jury, of course, and that just might make all the difference."

Aisha nodded her head. "If there's a different jury, does that mean at least one black person will be on it?"

I blinked. For some odd reason, I wasn't aware there wasn't a single black juror on this case. I internally kicked myself. That was the first thing I should've looked at. Instead, I was studying the trial transcripts, looking for any kind of prejudicial errors and looking at how poorly the attorney did with the case.

I suddenly felt my breath get labored. A United States Supreme Court case had just come down, settling this very question. In that United States Supreme Court case, *Flowers v. Mississippi*, the Court applied the *Batson* test. *Batson v. Kentucky* established in 1986 that a state may not use racially discriminatory reasons for peremptory challenges to jurors. In *Flowers*, the Supreme Court decided that all the black potential jurors had been eliminated by the prosecutor because of discriminatory intent. I would have to review the *Flowers* case more closely, because I had just skimmed it, but I remembered the Court looked at the fact that the potential black jurors had been stricken after having been asked many more questions than was asked of the white jurors, and that one black juror, in particular, had been stricken for reasons the white jurors were not. I believe the prosecutor made the excuse that the black juror worked at Wal-Mart, where the defendant's father also worked, and that she knew several defense witnesses. Other white jurors also knew people in the case, but they were not stricken by the state.

"Yes," I said slowly. "Yes, if there is a new trial, there will be other black people on the jury." I shook my head as I realized I might not succeed on a *Flower/Batson* argument if the trial attorney, Jim Stack, did not object to there not being any black jurors. I knew he probably didn't object, which meant the issue would not have been preserved. Still, I would have to request the *voir dire* and see exactly why no black jurors were impaneled on the case.

"That's good," Aisha said with a shake of her head. "Oh, lord, I couldn't believe no black folk managed to get on that jury. I don't know what that idiot attorney was thinking, letting the prosecutor get away with striking every single person of color."

"Every person of color was stricken?"

"Yeah, every one. There not only wasn't a black person on the jury, there wasn't a Hispanic or Asian or any kind of brown person, either. They were all lily white. Lily white and looking for blood from a poor black kid."

Well, that was interesting. I knew that in the *Batson* case and the *Flowers* case, the issue was that no African-Americans were on the jury. But in this case, everybody on the jury was white. Yes, apparently the attorney didn't object, but, as far as I was concerned, that was one more leg on which my ineffective assistance of counsel claim could stand.

"Is there anything else you can tell me about the case?" I asked her. "Anything that stood out to you at all?"

Aisha looked at the ceiling and then looked back at me. "No, I don't really know what to say. I mean, I was there the whole way, and I couldn't believe the things being allowed in by that idiot Jim Stack. But you can probably look at the trial transcripts and all that and you can see how bad he was."

It certainly was interesting that the jury was all-white. But could I make any kind of hay with that fact? I would simply have to try. Objection or no objection for the record, I would have to try.

I looked over at Aisha. She was hanging her head again. "I'm sorry," she said. "I started to have some hope that you can save my boy, but now, I just don't know. I don't want to ever start to think that Jamel will be out of prison, because hope is a killing thing. It's more killing than despair, if you want to know the truth. With despair, you know it. It's a feeling you're familiar with. You make your terms with it and you go on with your life. But if you got hope…well, if you got hope, then you suddenly have something to lose. You lose that light, that little bitty light that you allow into your bedroom at night. You start to depend on that light, and when it goes out, and everything is dark again, it's…"

Her voice trailed off and then she looked out the window again. The black and white cat, apparently sensing her mistress' sudden mood shift, decided to come over and comfort her. The enormous feline leaped down from the kitty tower onto the floor and then jumped up on Aisha's lap. It started to purr and rub her face on Aisha's arm, demanding that Aisha pet her. Aisha absently started to stroke the cat, her face a faraway mask. Just like she said, she dared not think that anything would come of this appeal. There would be nothing more devastating, I would imagine, than for her to believe and hope that she would see her son again in her home, that Jamel would one day be a free man, only to realize the appeal didn't do any good. I knew that the statistic of 12% was running through her head. It had to have been. The odds were against us, full stop, and both of us knew it.

"Well," she finally said. "I have to get ready for work. I have my Wal-Mart shift in a half hour and I'm going to be late as it is. Especially if the bus runs late, which it often does."

"I'm the reason you're running late. I would like to give you a ride to work."

"No, I couldn't put you out like that," she said.

"You're not putting me out," I said. "Please, I would like to do that for you."

"Well, if you're sure-"

"I'm sure."

The smile was back. But, unlike before, I could see the wariness behind the smile. The pain. The sleepless nights and the loneliness. The unbearable feeling that she had hopes for her son. Hopes and dreams that he would get married, give her grand-babies, have a good career and a home of his own. The same hopes any mother would have for her child. All those hopes were gone. Dashed by an incompetent attorney and an uncaring court.

Of course, she had been beaten down by life, long before her son was convicted for raping Felicity. It wasn't just the rape at the age of 15 and having her son through that rape. It was so many other injustices. Each aggression that was shown towards her in her life formed the cracks on her 33-year-old face, which made her seem older than her years.

She disappeared into the bedroom, and the black and white cat decided to grace me with its presence. I pet it absently while it purred and made bread on my lap. I looked at the clock and knew there wasn't much time for me to get Aisha to work on time. What would happen if she was late? Would she get a demerit? Would she be fired? What?

She came back out in a few minutes, dressed in a blue Wal-Mart frock with a white shirt underneath and khaki pants. "Thank you again for taking me to my job," she said. "I got a supervisor, she don't like it when folks are late. I had to take so much time off for Jamel's trial, I don't think I have much goodwill left at that store. You really saved me."

I smiled and put my arm around her instinctively. "It's my pleasure," I said.

The two of us drove to her store, which was only about 10 minutes away, and Aisha looked at her watch before getting out of the car. "Thank you very much, Christian," she said. "I know, I know, I shouldn't have hope. Hope is for other people. But God bless you anyway."

She kissed me on the cheek and then got out of the car and went into the store.

My heart was heavy as I drove away from her Wal-Mart. What had I gotten myself into? I bonded with this woman. I felt her pain in my heart.

If I lost this case, I would be that much more devastated now.

Chapter Eight

FELICITY

FELICITY MCDANIEL LOOKED out her window warily. She had been getting death threats lately and she knew her bodyguard might not be able to save her the next time. She took a deep breath, knowing that she was the only person who kept her secret.

She knew who had raped her. She knew it and couldn't tell a soul about who did it. If she did, she would be a dead woman.

It was hard for her, sitting at the trial for Jamel Jackson, knowing the poor kid was innocent. She wanted, so many times, to shout out loud to the judge that he was presiding over the wrong case. She wanted to shake the jury, brain the lame defense attorney who was drunk on the job. Nobody knew he was drunk, but Felicity did. She had grown up around enough alcoholics to know the signs. The too-long bathroom breaks that lame Jim Stack took, the "water bottle" he drank out of that Felicity knew was filled with straight vodka, the red face and bulbous nose on the man, the sweet smell on his breath that was masked by his cinnamon gum. He was a good one, though. He didn't stumble over his words, his eyes weren't bloodshot and his gait was sure. She was an expert on the tell-tale signs, though, because her father was a drunk and he did all the same things this Jim Stack did during the trial.

Yet she was afraid to go to the judge with her suspicions about Jim. She was afraid to do anything that would derail the proceedings, because she was warned that if she did, she would be a dead woman.

And she knew for a fact that the real rapist would kill her. He was an enormous man, powerful and angry all the time.

She was absolutely sick to her stomach when that poor Jamel was convicted. She wanted to shake that damn Jim Stack, pummel her fists into his skull and force him to actually give that kid a decent defense. She just couldn't believe he didn't do anything for that kid at all. Of course, her rapist was happy when Jamel was convicted for what he did. He was thrilled because it meant he got away with it.

She touched her face where she could feel the faintest of scars. It wasn't really there anymore, for she had the best plastic surgeon in the world work on her. She didn't really have a choice in the matter because she was unconscious when the plastic surgeons were working on her, but, when she finally came-to, she had to have Dr. Matagari finish the job. He was known to be the best. He had worked on friends of hers in the industry and they always were very happy with his work. They all said he made them look refreshed, as opposed to plastic, and he never drastically changed a person's face, like what had happened to the late Kenny Rogers under the knife.

The fact that she looked like herself again after what that monster had done to her was a cold comfort. She had seen pictures of what she had looked like in the hospital when she was brought in, before the swelling had gone down enough that the doctors could work their magic, and she was still appalled at what she had seen in those pictures. One of her eyes was completely closed with a huge lump of swelling over it. She looked like Rocky Balboa after he went 10 rounds with Apollo Creed and his trainer had to slit his eye open with a razor. Her other eye was bruised and deep black, while her mouth was slit so that she looked like The Joker. Her entire face was swollen, for that matter. In looking at the pictures, she was surprised she fared as well as she did.

Yes, she looked like herself again, whatever that meant. She never felt she was attractive, even though everybody else always told her how beautiful she was. She thought she was more interesting-looking than anything else. Her eyes were too close together, her nose was a tad too long, her lips were just a smidgen too wide. She was too gangly, too bony, too tall. Of course, the fact that she didn't have cookie-cutter looks helped her immensely when she first started modeling. She didn't even have to go to the modeling cattle calls that other girls did – a scout found her one day when she was sitting outside a coffee shop with her dog. The scout decided she was the future face of Cover Girl, and, before she knew it, she had made a household name for herself in the magazines. The *Sports Illustrated* swimsuit edition cover soon followed, and, after that, came the movies.

She surprised herself about how much she enjoyed making movies. She figured she would hate it, much like she hated all the time spent on hair and makeup before a photo shoot. Nothing drove her more crazy than to have to just sit there while this person blew out her frizzy hair so that it was smooth as silk, while that person fussed over her with various brushes and wands. She would do a shoot then have to sit in that damned chair for another three hours for a different shoot. It was all the ninth circle of hell to her, but making movies, that was a different thing. She was a natural at it, and, before she knew it, she was being nominated for Emmys for her work on various Netflix limited series. She even made feature films, mainly indies, because she found the independent movie scripts to be just so much more fulfilling than the big studios, but she also made quite a few big studio films.

And if it weren't for the monster who attacked her, she would have to say that she had lived a charmed life. Everything fell into her lap. She didn't have to work for much of anything. Her modeling career, her acting career, all of it.

But what had angered the monster - she didn't dare speak his name, even to herself, because speaking his name, even in her head, somehow conjured him up for her and terrified her, so she simply had to refer to him as "the monster" - was that she was secretly a lesbian. She had men over to her house, mainly because she wanted her neighbors to think she was some kind of a loose woman with the men and they would leave her alone, but she really preferred women. And the monster couldn't handle that one.

"You like women?" he asked when he persisted in asking her out on a date, time and again.

"Yes I do," she simply said. "Trust me, when I reject you, it's nothing personal. I mean, look at you. You're gorgeous. Anybody would like to go out with you. Anybody who's into men, that is, which I'm not. So-"

At that, he slapped her for the first time.

"Don't lie to me, bitch. I know you see a lot of guys over here. You think I'm stupid? I'm not stupid. I know for a fact that you have guys over here all the time, you fucking whore."

Felicity was terrified of him from that point on. But, no matter what she did, she just could not get rid of him. Nothing worked to deter him. She took out a restraining order against him, but that didn't work, because he was too well-connected. He would literally violate a restraining order and come to her house and nobody did a thing about it, because of who he was. He was never going to get arrested for anything he did. Once Felicity found out exactly what kind of monster he was, what he'd been doing over his life, all the women he had raped and left for dead, and had never been arrested for any of it – Felicity knew who she was dealing with. He was like the Mercury man in the Terminator movie - no matter what people tried to do to him, he always reconstituted himself and came charging right back.

Since she was a highly regarded actress, she figured that maybe she could try to use her power in the industry to make sure he left her alone. Felicity was stunned to find out her power and prestige in the industry meant absolutely nothing. Nobody would protect her, because again, he was just too important.

Or, as one studio head had put it to her – "you'll just have to put up with it. Sorry, nobody is going to do anything about him. He's been a problem for years and he's going to continue to be a problem. You're just going to have to find a way to deal with it. Unless, of course, you want to commit professional suicide. If that's your bag, be my guest. Just don't ever say my fingerprints are on any of it. Best that I don't get caught holding the knife."

"Thanks a lot, Alex ," Felicity said to the studio head

whom she had spoken with about the monster. "I knew you would be on my side."

He just shrugged. "I'm on the side of keeping my job. Period, end of story. And if you cross that guy, you'll be on the street. Again, if that's your bag, I say go for it. As for me, I'm not going to be on the street with you. You can ask around, ask anybody you want to help you. Nobody will."

So, the upshot was that Felicity had to put up with the monster constantly coming over to her home, unannounced, and threatening her. Most of the time, he left without laying a hand on her. But there were other times when she had to have sex with him because it was either that or he would rape her. She figured out that actually pretending she was into him was one good way of placating him just a little bit, just enough that he would not harm her physically. She figured that was the lesser of the two evils – either have sex with him or have him beat and rape her if she refused.

It was excruciating for her to do that, however. It was excruciating for her not just because she couldn't stand the sight of him, even though he was extremely handsome. Classically handsome, tall, broad and built, with big dark eyes, black hair, chiseled face, and huge dimples. And a huge something else, too, which actually was not a good thing in her case, because she didn't want that in the first place. He usually took it from her when she was not wet for him, so the pain was excruciating.

Despite the fact that he was a walking Calvin Klein model, with an eight pack, she could not stand the sight of him. It was like when she always read about how Satan would appear when he came to earth - he would appear as a beautiful angel, because that's what he was up in heaven. He wouldn't have horns, or a tail, he would not be ugly, or fulfill any of the stereotypes Hollywood foisted upon the unsuspecting public. No, when Satan finally appeared to the world, he would appear just like this monster does.

For a while, Felicity actually was convinced he was Satan. He just seemed to so invincible, so impenetrable. It seemed to Felicity that there was nothing that could bring him down.

Unfortunately, because of what happened to her, with him beating her and leaving her for dead, raping her like that, Felicity had been unable to work. She felt that was career suicide anyway, because if you don't work steadily, people forget about you. That was the ironic thing about this entire ordeal – she didn't want to make any waves against him while he was harassing her, coming over and beating her and raping her, so she took the studio head's advice and did not go public with what he was doing. Now she wished she had done that, even if it meant certain death for her. She should have been brave enough to tell the world what she knew about him, instead of letting poor Jamel go to prison for what this man did. If she would've just had a bit of courage, none of that would've happened. Not that she thought the monster would ever go behind bars. She didn't dare hope for that. But, at least, there would be the chance he would be publicly humiliated for what he was doing, not to mention what he had done to women over the years.

But now it was too late. She started to obsessively find out what it would take to win an appeal when a kid is duly convicted like Jamel was in a court of law. She realized the odds were extremely long that Jamel would ever see the outside of the prison wall, only 12%, and, even so, it didn't matter that he was factually innocent. She had her chance to testify in court against the monster and on behalf of poor

Jamel, but she didn't do it when she had the chance. So now, it was what it was. One life was devastated, well, no, that wasn't necessarily true. It wasn't just Jamel's life that had been devastated, but the lives of everybody around him, everybody who cared about him. It's never just one life devastated when something like this happens. The blast radius can go for miles. But she had to try not to think about that. If she really got down in the weeds and thought about all the people hurt by what happened to her at the hands of the monster, she would never be able to sleep again.

Not that she was sleeping now.

Chapter Nine

CHRISTIAN

ONCE I FOUND out from Aisha that there were no blacks or people of color on the jury against Jamel, I knew that I had to speak with Jim Stack, so I made an appointment with him. He was no longer at the public defender's office, but was in private practice, no doubt taking people's money and not delivering anything to them. After all, he didn't deliver anything to Jamel - why would he start being a good attorney now?

When I made an appointment to see him, he knew exactly what I wanted from him. I was sure he knew about the appeal. I expected him to be defensive when I called him, and to shut me down, but he was not.

"I have an opening tomorrow at two on my schedule. You can come to my office then."

So I found myself going to his office in Studio City. He had a storefront, and, as I looked in the window at his suite, I realized he probably was not doing very well for himself. I walked in and there was a metal desk in the middle of the room and a couple of threadbare couches in the waiting area. Other than that, there was not really a whole lot in this office. I looked to my right and saw Jim talking on the phone in his small office, and, from the other office just down the hall – it seemed this suite only had two offices – I could hear somebody screaming at the top of his lungs at his computer. He was cussing at it, saying every word he knew at the computer, as if the computer would start working magically because of his words. While I definitely could relate to his frustrations, as anybody who owns a computer could relate, I definitely could not relate to screaming and yelling at the top of my lungs at an inanimate object.

"Goddamn you mother fucking piece of shit," the other attorney down the hall was screaming. "I am so tired of this goddamn piece of crap computer. I swear to God, I'm going to throw it out the window at any second."

I smiled a little as I flipped through the magazines waiting for Jim to finish his conversation. He finally did, then he came out to the waiting room and shook my hand.

"Hi, I'm Jim Stack. I guess you're Christian and you're doing the appeal for Jamel Jackson?" He was smiling and his body language was open. As was the collar of his shirt, which was a short-sleeve button-down with a collar that buttoned to the shirt. I imagined he probably got it at Walmart.

At least, that was kind of my impression. His shirt definitely did not look expensive nor did it look professional. Neither did his polyester brown pants nor his scuffed-up leather shoes. He was holding a cup of coffee when he came out of the office and his eyes were bloodshot. He led me into his tiny, cramped office, where I could see that, in addition to the metal desk, a couple of threadbare chairs, and a Formica bookshelf, which he probably put together from

IKEA, there was also a small cot in there. He motioned to the cot and looked embarrassed about it. "This is just temporary. I'm looking for a place to land. My wife finally kicked me out."

I got a whiff of his coffee cup, and I understood exactly why his wife probably kicked him out. The coffee was definitely laced with some kind of alcohol - bourbon, from the smell of it. My stomach started to turn over just a little bit, just because I could not imagine drinking before noon. It was presently 10:30 in the morning. Of course, it was 5 o'clock somewhere, but I did not imagine that would be a good excuse for this guy to be drinking at this hour.

I sat down and so did he. He clasped his hands in front of him as he looked at me with his bloodshot eyes. "What can I do for you?"

"As you no doubt are aware, I've taken the case of Jamel Jackson's appeal from his criminal conviction. I just wanted to warn you, at the present moment, I'm going to be relying on an ineffective assistance of counsel defense. I just wanted to give you a heads-up about that. I also wanted to ask you, point-blank, why you did such a poor job on this kid's case."

He nodded, as if he knew this appeal would be coming down the pike at some point.

"I was having personal issues at that time," he said. "I was drinking all through the trial and I didn't know what I was doing during it, because, I'll be honest with you, half the time I did not even know where I was. Hit me with the points you think I did wrong. I'm sure I probably did a lot of wrong, because I'll be the first to admit that I dropped the ball on that kid's case. If it helps you at all, I'll have you know that I am no longer working for the public defender's office, and the reason why am no longer working for them is because of Jamel's case."

That didn't surprise me. Of course he wasn't working for the public defender's office. He was working here in this shitty place as a one-man fuck-up band.

"Go on," I said.

"I'm sure that you think I'm a fuck up," he said, reading my mind. "A wastoid. I'm not going to argue the point about that, because I am those things. But I wasn't always like that. I wasn't always like that at all. I mean, I always knew alcoholism was in my genes. My father and my mother both were a couple of drunks and so were their parents. So you might say that I've come from a long line of alcoholics. But I always tried very hard to not become like them. I didn't take a drink until I was 30 years old."

I somehow couldn't believe that. This guy seemed like the sort who started drinking at the age of 11 and just never stopped.

"I know about you," he continued. "When you called me, I did a little background check on you. I found out you used to work for a white shoe firm in San Diego, making the big bucks. I want you to know that I, too, worked for a white shoe firm here in Los Angeles before I became like this. I was working for a big entertainment firm. We had clients you wouldn't believe. Big celebrities, models, actors and actresses, directors, studio heads, you name it, we represented them. Sports stars, too. I was making the big bucks. But I started drinking, and then I started using and I lost all my money in the Las Vegas casinos. Turns out it's true what they say about an addict – if you have an addictive personality, you're going to be addicted to a lot of different things. And once I decided to let the devil in, it was Katie bar the door. I took a sip of wine at a celebration the partners had for landing an enormous account of a very prominent actress. If I told you who it was, you would be astounded.

A-list does not even cover what this actress is to this town. She's a legend and our firm landed her. I decided at that point that I had never taken a drink in my entire life, and everybody was drinking champagne, and I did not want to have a sip of even that. But later on that night, I had a glass of wine. That one glass of wine turned something on inside of me, I don't know, I guess it was maybe a latent desire, but it was very strong. After that first glass of wine, I lost myself in the bottle."

A sad story, one I'd heard many times before. While I felt for this guy, I was still angry that he messed up Jamel's case so completely.

"That's when I also started to use cocaine, mainly because I had to when I appeared in court," he said. "I would be so drunk that I could barely stand up so I needed to do some lines to perk me back up. Just to make me alert in court. The gambling came later. That, too, was something that must've always been inside me, the demon that wanted to go to Las Vegas and could never stay away from any of the tables. I was drinking and using, but the partners in my firm didn't know that at that point, so all of us took a trip to Vegas. It was another celebratory thing and the senior partner was paying for everything that weekend. I tried to stay away from the casinos because I just knew that if I did not stay away that I would get lost at the tables just like I got lost in the bottle. But the siren song was just too strong. I went down to play some slots. Nobody saw me for the entire weekend because I could not leave the casinos. I came back every single weekend. I told myself that I was only trying to win back the money I lost and that if I ever could get to the point where I was in the black, I would just walk away."

Again, that was a familiar story people always told

themselves. *Just win back everything I've lost so that I at least break even and then I'll walk away.* At some point, the law of sunk costs kicks in and nobody can walk away, because it was always virtually impossible to break even. That was the mind of a gambling addict, and, apparently, that was the mind of Jim as well.

"But of course, that did not happen," Jim said. "I didn't walk away after I won big enough to cover my previous losses. I won a big jackpot, and, at that point, that jackpot was enough to cover my previous gambling expenses and a little more. But all that Jackpot did for me was make me try to hit it again, and again, and again. And then I started playing blackjack, poker, craps, Baccarat, you name it. I wasn't very good at any of it. It did not help that I was drinking and using while I was doing all of this. Six months later, I had a nest egg that was completely gone. $1,000,000, gone, in just six months. So I started embezzling from the firm and lost my license to practice law when the partners found out about it and turned me in, and then, when I got my license back - it was only suspended, I was not disbarred - I got a job with the public defender's office. I was grateful for that job, even though it was a huge step down for me income-wise and prestige -wise."

I was taken aback a little bit by how much this guy was willing to admit to me about his life. I knew he was trying to make excuses as to why he did such a poor job on Jamel's case. I didn't really know where he was going with any of it, considering he was still drinking. It wasn't like he could say to me that he did all this and now here he was, whole and well, because that was not the case. He definitely was neither whole nor well.

I decided just let him tell me the rest of it.

"I was hit with this murder case, and I wasn't gambling

anymore, because I was going to gambling anonymous, but I was still drinking. By that time, however, I was able to cover it up a little bit. When you drink enough, you start to handle your liquor in a way. You can still get messed up, so messed up that you don't know what you're doing, but you can at least modify your behavior so that nobody knows how wasted you really are. And that's the point I got to in Jamel's case. I got to the point where I was drinking, getting loaded every single day, but nobody was ever the wiser about it."

I wondered about that. If he was drinking that much, why would the judge put up with it? Apparently, however, he was able to cover it up enough that maybe the judge didn't realize what was happening.

"I know that I didn't do a good job with his case," Jim went on. "Like I said, I was having a lot of personal problems during this time, too. A lot of stuff was coming up for me, because my dad died right before this trial began. When he died, it was like the floodgate had opened. I was dealing with a lot of grief about that, about how I could never make amends with him again. We weren't speaking when he died and hadn't been speaking for years. I blamed him for my mother's death, years ago, because she died of cirrhosis of the liver and I always thought he was got her drinking. And I just blamed him for being a shitty father. Which he definitely was. I blamed him for my drinking problem, my drug problem, my gambling problem. I blamed him for all of that, because that's what I grew up around. That's all I knew."

So, it was the perfect storm. A drunk gets hit with a tragedy, right before trial began. No wonder he was such a mess. That didn't excuse it, but I knew it would be helpful to me when I asked for my evidentiary hearing on the issue of ineffective assistance of counsel.

"The last thing I wanted to do was try a case, let alone a major rape case involving a high-profile actress, but that's what I had to do," he continued on. "I phoned it in. I'll admit that. I not only phoned it in, but I barely could stay on my feet at all during the trial. So that's why I did not put on any evidence on his behalf, and that's why I just let the prosecutor strike every single person of color off the jury - I did not want to argue with the prosecutor about his peremptory strikes. I did not have the energy to go to the court and tell them those peremptory strikes were not appropriate, to say the least. I just let him strike everybody of color off the jury. And yes, I knew, looking back, that there was quite a bit of evidence the prosecutor got in that should not have ever come in. I didn't challenge the things that came in. I never made the argument that a small boy like Jamel couldn't have gotten on Felicity's grounds without some help. If I was any kind of an attorney, I would have brought in pictures of the high stone wall that led to her house and the stone wall that led to her pool area, and evidence that the pool area was supposed to have been locked with a combination lock that Jamel could not possibly have known. I just let the prosecutor get away with the argument that Jamel just came off the street, went back there and raped her and left her for dead, and then called 911."

"Yeah, that never did make sense to me," I said. "If he actually raped her, why would he also be the one to call the ambulance and wait there with her?"

"That did not make sense to me, but somehow, the prosecutor was able to explain that away," he said. "He explained to the jury that the theory was that Jamel raped her and then called the ambulance because he was concerned she would die, and if she died, he would be charged with murder on top of the rape charge, so he knew he had to call the ambulance right away. They never explained how he would've been caught if he fled the scene. That was always a hole in the entire case and I did not even bother to plug it in."

This guy was confessing everything and I appreciated it.

"I guess after talking with you, I'm going to have to file a writ as soon as possible, and get into court as soon as possible," I said. "I'm going to have a judiciary hearing on everything you just told me, and I'm sorry, I know you probably don't want to be thrown under the bus like this, but this could be the only way I can get this kid out of prison. I'm hoping the appeals court can hear this as soon as possible and maybe overturn the conviction and order a new trial. I'm very sorry, but after what you told me, I really don't think there is any more of a clear-cut case of ineffective assistance of counsel. I know this will put you in the crosshairs of the California bar, again, but I really don't see any choice."

He nodded. He knew he was defeated. "Listen, I know what you're saying, and I can say that there has not been a night that has gone by since Jamel was convicted that I have not laid awake thinking about it. I feel terrible about what happened to that poor kid. Just awful. So, yes, I'll do whatever you need me to. If you need to have an evidentiary hearing on a writ, then apply for that writ and I'll show up for the hearing. I will tell the judge what I told you. I have nothing to hide. I mean, as you probably know, I'm still drinking. That has not changed. But there might be a way that I can have a little bit of peace of mind if I could help get that kid out of jail."

I took a deep breath, knowing I would have to approach this appeal in a much different way than I thought I would have to in the first place. I would have to file a writ of *habeas corpus*, as I could not present evidence about the ineffective assistance of counsel to the appellate court on a regular appeal because the appellate court would only review mistakes that court might've made. That was not going to get me to where I wanted to go, but this probably would.

It was still long shot, but it was less of a long shot than it was before.

Chapter Ten

CHRISTIAN

I HAD to tell my law student that I would have to go exclusively with case law that would help me with my ineffective assistance of counsel claim and that she would have to help me prepare a writ of *habeas corpus* so that I could get Jamel out of prison as soon as possible and get this matter before an appellate court. So I filed my writ. My student and I did research for the better part of the weekend, and I waited for the opportunity to hopefully have a hearing on the writ.

TWO WEEKS LATER, I got my answer – the appellate court was willing to hear what I had to say about the ineffective assistance of counsel, and it set an evidentiary hearing for the following week. I was immediately giddy beyond measure. I knew from my research that writs are not easy to win, and I didn't believe this one would be easy, either, but at least I was getting a shot. The appellate court did not necessarily even have to grant an evidentiary hearing on this matter, so I knew the petition I'd put into the court was good. I knew it was well-researched, based upon facts, and I had included an affidavit from Jim in my petition, along with as much case law as I possibly could find on the matter.

So now it was up to me to put Jim on the stand to admit to the court about his problems during the trial and hope for the best. If this writ of *habeas corpus* did not succeed, I still had the notice of appeal out, and I could still try to appeal the case on other grounds. However, I still was having trouble finding anywhere that the court had erred during the trial, so I did not believe that would've gone very far. In other words, it was either win on an Ineffective Assistance of Counsel claim or bust.

I called Avery to tell her the good news about the evidentiary hearing I would be getting on my writ, and she was ecstatic.

"What happens if your writ is granted?" she asked.

"Well, here's what happens. The appellate court could just order him released, which I don't think will happen, or, probably more likely, he will order a new trial. But, if Jamel gets new trial, at least we're still in the game. Avery, I reviewed the transcript for this case exhaustively, and I really believe that if Jamel gets a proper attorney on his retrial, he'll win. He'll be acquitted. I just know it."

"Well, good luck." She paused for a few minutes. "When are you coming back down to San Diego again?"

I'd been in Los Angeles for the better part of the past two weeks, feverishly working on Jamel's writ of *habeas corpus*. I knew my San Diego cases were suffering because of it, but it could not be helped. I'd thrown myself into this case, wholeheartedly, and there was just no way I could possibly not give it my all. Especially after meeting Aisha and Jamel himself.

When I told Aisha that the appellate court had agreed to hear evidence on my writ, she was over the moon. But I could also tell that she was wary not to get her hopes up again. I told her that even if the appellate court reversed the trial court's decision because of the ineffective assistance of counsel, we were not out of the woods yet. We had to probably go through another trial, and that would be hard on everybody involved. But I hoped to come up with evidence, or Regina could come up with evidence, about who the real perpetrator was in this case, and there would be the possibility that I could convince a prosecutor not to bring another case against Jamel, if the evidence I found was compelling enough.

So, that night, I was working at my office late when I got a phone call from somebody.

That somebody was Felicity McDaniel herself.

Chapter Eleven

CHRISTIAN

I MADE an appointment for Felicity to see me. I was excited to be talking to her, but I did not necessarily know what kind of evidence she would give to me. According to the trial transcripts, she did not even take the stand. She had told the prosecutors that she had no memory or recollection of what happened to her that night, she had no idea who raped and beat her, and she had nothing to say on her behalf. So the prosecutor did not even bother to call her to the stand. So while I found it curious that she would be contacting me, I was not necessarily thinking that she would have any new information for me that would be helpful. Nevertheless, I knew I would have to talk to her and see what she had to say.

She came in to see me the following day. I was struck by how she looked. They always say that pictures don't do these actresses and models justice, and that was certainly the case with Felicity. I always thought she was a beautiful woman when I saw her in the movies and in magazines, but nothing could prepare me for the way she looked in person.

The only thing I could really say about her was that she glowed. Her skin was a perfect milky white, with not a line present on her face at all. It was as smooth as a baby's skin. Her eyes were multicolored, a mix of bright green and blue, with a little tiny bit of hazel around the iris, and they were framed by lush dark eyelashes. Her face was sculpted, her lips were full, her neck swan-like, her bearing regal. Her blonde hair was straight, thick and perfectly styled. When she walked into my office, it was as if she were a panther stalking its prey - she was so lithe and graceful that she took my breath away.

I read a little about her in the tabloids and magazines, and I discovered that she did not seek out modeling jobs. The scout found her sitting outside a coffee shop and the rest was history. Neither did she seek out acting jobs. Her agent sent her to one gig and she got it immediately, a starring role in a major motion picture. Ever since then, she was one of the most highly sought after actors in Hollywood. Most actresses and models would have been terribly jealous of this woman because she did not have to do anything that most of them had to do. The cattle calls, the humiliations in front of studio heads and modeling agencies, none of that. She just fell into jobs because she was that beautiful and that talented.

And, she was breathtaking. Absolutely breathtaking.

And yet, she had a certain vulnerability that really shown through when she sat down in front of me and clutched her purse in front of her tightly with white knuckles. Her nails were perfect and painted white, and, when she sat there in front of me, not saying a word, she was biting her lower lip while looking down at my desk.

"Ms. McDaniel, you wanted to see me?" I asked, breaking the ice.

She nodded her head. "Yes. I need to talk to you. I know you have Jamel Jackson's case, and I heard through the grapevine that you're going to have a hearing on whether or not he should stay in prison. What kind of hearing is it again?"

I cleared my throat. "It's called a hearing on a writ of *habeas corpus*. Basically, the appellate court has scheduled an evidentiary hearing on whether or not Jamel had ineffective assistance of counsel, so much so that if the counsel would've not been ineffective, Jamel would've been acquitted in this case. That's what I need to show. Not just that his counsel wasn't effective, but also that he would have been acquitted, but-for the counsel being so terrible. It's still a long shot, don't get me wrong, but it's the only shot we have."

She nodded. "I hope you win. I really do." She carefully tucked some strands of her blonde hair behind her ear and then she nervously gripped her purse tighter in front of her. I could see her swallowing. I could see her breathing hard.

"You hope I win?"

She nodded again. "Yes. I really hope you win."

"So you don't think he raped you?" Why did I think that she did not have memory loss as to what happened that night? Jamel had been convicted for raping her and if she really didn't know who had done it, I wouldn't think she would be on my side. She would have believed that Jamel had raped her, because that's what the evidence showed and that's what the jury found beyond a reasonable doubt.

At least that's what the prosecutor's evidence showed. The defense attorney did not show any evidence at all.

She shook her head. "No. I do not believe he raped me. That's what I wanted to talk to you about. What happens if you win on this case?"

"If I win on the writ, Jamel might be released completely. Although I don't think that'll happen. That would be my dream, of course. But most likely, if I win on the writ, he'll be tried again. At that time, I will take over the helms on his retrial. So, hopefully, with any luck, Jamel will be acquitted."

"I don't know," she said. "I mean, I don't think you know what you're dealing with here. Who you're dealing with here. Is there any way possible that Jamel would not have to go through another trial?"

"Do you know more than you told the cops about who did this to you?" I blurted out.

She didn't say anything which spoke volumes to me. "Listen, you didn't answer my question," she said, instead of answering *my* question. "Is there any way possible Jamel won't have to go through another trial?"

"Yes. As I said earlier, there is a possibility that if I win on the writ of *habeas corpus*, the appellate court will just order the trial court reversed and not remanded, which means Jamel will be free. He will be released, but, as I said, I don't think this case will happen that way. We're going to have to go through a new trial. I'm sure of it. And even if the judge reverses the trial court and does not remand, the prosecutor can still re-file the charges against Jamel. Nothing precludes that. So, I would say there's a 99.9% chance that there will be a new trial, even if I win on my writ."

She started to breathe very hard. "Here's the thing. If he goes through a new trial, and he's acquitted, he's in danger. You're in danger. I'm in danger. Everybody's in danger."

So she did know who did this to her and she was terrified of him. "Be that as it may, I'm sorry, but I think you know for a fact that my client did not do this. If he did not do this, he has to have another chance to show the court his innocence. The only way he's going to get that chance is if I win on a writ. I know you're trying to tell me something about the real person who did this, but I can't let that deter me. I hope you understand."

"No, I hope *you* understand," she said. She lowered her voice, but there was a frantic quality about it, a panic. "There's a reason I did not tell the court the truth about what happened to me. I had to sit there and see that poor kid get convicted for something somebody else did. Believe me, it was hardest thing I've ever had to do. I've not been able to sleep ever since then. But I knew I had no choice. If I would've told the truth, I would not be sitting here in front of you. I would be dead." She blinked. "All I can say is that you have to step very lightly with this case. Be very careful. Because if you're not, you will be disappeared. So will Jamel. And so will I."

This was about the oddest thing I'd ever experienced. "I don't understand."

"You will. I'm sorry. It's all I can really say to you, except for that you will find out what I'm talking about." She looked around the office, as if she was afraid the person who she was talking about with me was around somewhere. Maybe he was.

"Listen, if you know something, which I know you do, you need to tell me who did this. As I said, I think there's a good chance I can get the conviction overturned. But when it comes to getting a new trial, it's going to be a whole new ballgame. I'm going to need your testimony. It's going to be crucial. In fact, if you talk to the prosecutor, and you told him —"

When I said the words "the prosecutor," she seemed to shiver. Her face got very white. "I really want you to listen to me. This is a very dangerous man. I suppose Jim Stack told you that during the trial, or right before the trial, his father died? He told you that, didn't he?"

"Yeah, he did. He told me his father died right before the trial began. Why?"

"Do you think it's a coincidence that the attorney for Jamel was somebody like Jim Stack? Somebody who was on the edge to begin with? Someone who had a lot of personal problems with addictions, not just drinking and drugs, but gambling?"

"I don't know what you're getting at. After all, he was working at the public defender's office at the time. I assumed he was just given the case by the head of the public defender's office and that was that. I didn't think there was anything to it."

"If you don't think there's anything to it, then I don't know what to say to you. I'm trying to tell you something here. I'm also trying to tell you that it was not a coincidence that his father died before the trial. You have to listen to what I'm saying to you here."

"Are you saying that Jim Stack's father was killed?"

"I'm not saying that at all," she said, although I knew she was saying just that. "I just want to tell you that what happened to Jim Stack's father right before the trial was that he was killed by a mugger on the street. He was held up at gunpoint and he apparently gave the guy his wallet, but the guy shot them anyway. It was known in the legal community that Jim Stack had a problem. Honestly, I don't know why he was ever hired by the public defender's office in the first place. Maybe there's a story behind that one as well, but I don't know. But it was known that Jim was having a lot of problems with addiction, so, when his father died right before the trial, what do you think would've happened? Do you think the guy on the edge, who just lost his father, will give anybody a good defense? The answer to that is pretty simple. No. And he should have been taken off the case when his father was murdered like that. But he wasn't. I don't know, maybe he told his superiors that he could muddle through, but obviously he couldn't. All that I can say is that there is a powerful force who wanted to make sure Jim Stack defended Jamel Jackson in this case, and they wanted to make sure Jim Stack had so many issues during that time that he would be completely checked out. And I can also tell you another thing – you weren't supposed to be on this case. Nobody was supposed to be on this case. What was supposed to have happened was that Jamel couldn't afford to hire somebody to write a writ of *habeas corpus*, or an appeal, and he was supposed to spend the rest of his life behind bars. Now, here you are, taking the case. Which I think is great. But you're messing with their plans."

"Who do you mean when you say 'their' plans? Are you saying there is more than one person involved in this?"

"I'm saying there's a lot of people involved with this. A lot of people are very interested in making sure a certain person never pays for the crimes he perpetrates on women. That he has perpetrated on women for years. Trust me, it's like a coven of witches around him. It's like that movie *The Omen*, where that crazy lady screams 'it's all for you, Damien,' right before she jumps off the roof. This case goes beyond the good old boy network. It goes way beyond that. I don't want to tell you to drop this appeal. I don't want that poor kid to spend the rest of his life in prison. I really don't know what to do here. I've been put into this terrible dilemma, where I can't live with the shame and guilt of a kid like that Jamel being in prison. I mean, I studied him while I was at the trial and he seems like such a nice kid. A good egg. And he saved my life. I can't discount that at all. If he did not save my life by calling 911, he would've never gotten into this position in the first place. A lot of kids in his situation, seeing a woman like me near death by the pool, they would just run, because they did not want to get involved. But he did not run. He called 911 and I was saved." She shook her head. "He sacrificed himself for me. That's not lost on me, believe it."

Her delicate white fingers were tapping on my desk and she was shaking all over. She started to cry and I silently pushed my box of Kleenex over to her. She gratefully took a handful and dabbed her eyes.

"Listen, I know what you're saying," I said. "And I can't force you to testify if there's a new trial. I mean, I could subpoena you, but I can't force you to tell the truth. I get a sense that if there is a new trial, and I subpoena you, you're going to lie on the stand just because you're terrified. I get that. But I have to do what I have to do. What I was hired to do. I met both Jamel and his mother - these are two completely lost souls. I simply cannot stand by and let that kid languish in prison. He needs to live a normal life just like everybody else. He needs to experience the joy of having his own children, a home of his own, a job of his own, a wife of his own. He needs to have dinners with his mother and help her when she's old. He needs to take his future kids to Disneyland and to the beach on weekends. He needs to have a full life. He does not deserve to be in prison. And that's all I know. I know you're telling me that if I go forward with this case that my life might be in danger. So be it. I have to do what I know is right. Otherwise, I don't think I could sleep at night. I could not look at myself in the mirror again."

By this time, Felicity was wringing the Kleenex in her

hands. "I understand. I felt it was my duty to warn you about what you're getting into. And, it's also my duty to tell you that, as I said before, you're not the only one whose life will be in danger if this goes too far. It's going to be mine and Jamel's."

I took a deep breath. "I hate to say it, because I know that what I'm going to do is going to affect your life. But, as I said before. So be it."

Chapter Twelve

CHRISTIAN

TWO WEEKS LATER, I got into court, which was an evidentiary hearing for my writ of *habeas corpus*. Jamel was in the courtroom with me, because he was out on the writ. Of course, he was probably going to have to go back to prison after the hearing, unless, by some miracle, the judge decided to overturn the conviction right then and there. However, I was bracing for him to deny the application for the writ completely. And, barring that, the best I could hope for would be to have the entire case reversed and remanded, at which point I would have to get ready for Jamel's trial.

Jim Stack was there too. He was the indispensable witness I would call to show what happened to Jamel.

"Dog, what do you think is going to happen today?" Jamel asked me nervously. He was still in his prison garb, although he was not shackled. But he was being guarded very closely.

"Well, as I told you before, I'm going to have Mr. Stack testify on why it was he did what he did. After that, it's up to the judge. It's the best I can do."

The appellate judge was named Judge Warner. He was the Los Angeles County District Court Judge. The prosecutor was the same prosecutor who tried the case – Matthew Howard. He was a cocky son of a bitch - I had heard about his reputation from some of the attorneys I spoke with. I couldn't stand the sight of him. I had to wonder if maybe Matthew was in on the whole case.

The judge called the case to order and he asked me to make my argument.

I stood up, introduced myself, and went through the caselaw I found on the issue of ineffective assistance of counsel and also on the issue of not having any people of color on the jury.

"I'd like to object to any kind of argument about the makeup of the jury," Matthew said to the judge. "The record shows that the defense counsel did not object to the makeup of the jury in front of the trial court, therefore the issue was forever waived. It was not preserved for an appeal."

"Your Honor, I understand there was no objection to the makeup of the jury. However, in light of the fact that the Supreme Court has ruled in numerous cases that not having members of one's own race on a jury can be a violation of an individual's constitutional rights, I believe it is such an important matter that even if there was no objection on the record, this court should still consider it. Bear in mind that the Supreme Court cases which have dealt with this have dealt specifically with the matter of an individual's specific race, but in this case, everybody on this jury was white. I would think that such an egregious example of violating my client's constitutional rights should shock the conscience."

"Be that as it may," Matthew said. "It was not preserved."

"And, Your Honor," I began. "Another reason why I bring it up is because it shows the counsel was ineffective. It's important that this court know about this particular point, because, as I'm sure your honor is aware, the test for whether or not the case should be overturned for ineffective assistance of counsel is two-pronged. The first prong is that the counsel was ineffective. And I need to show that with the testimony of the counsel in question, Jim Stack. The second prong is that the outcome would've been different if the counsel was not ineffective. In this case, because the counsel was ineffective, and he failed to object about the fact the jury did not have a single black member, or a person of color on it, that is just one way the outcome would have been different if the counsel was effective. I believe it's important to bring the situation of the jury to light."

"I will allow the argument about the makeup of the jury to enter the record, and I will consider it when I make my decision," Judge Warner said. "You may proceed."

Score one for me.

After I made my opening argument, and so did Matthew, it was time for me to call Jim Stack to take the stand.

"Can you please state your name for the record?" I said to him after he was sworn in.

"James Robert Stack," he said.

"Now, we are in front of the Court of Appeals for Los Angeles County today on a writ of *habeas corpus*. We are here to present evidence to the court about an ineffective assistance of counsel claim. To that end, I would like to ask you a few questions."

And then, for the next hour so, I broke him down. He was willing, and ready, to testify about what he did in that case, or what he did not do.

"Did you object to the makeup of the jury?" I asked him.

"No."

"Were there any African-Americans available for jury duty for this case?"

"Yes. There were 30 different African-American men and women available for jury duty. But none of them served because they were all stricken through peremptory challenges."

"And did you object to every single one of them being stricken?"

"No."

"And why did you not object to that?"

"I did not object to that, because, quite frankly, I did not even realize there was not a single black member on the jury. Not until they were seated and I looked at them and realized what had happened."

"And how did you not realize that all people of color were stricken?"

"I didn't realize it because I was not paying attention. And, quite frankly, I was wasted throughout the entire trial. I didn't even know what was going on half the time."

At that, he told the judge the entire sad story about his addictions, about his father dying, and about how he was phoning it in throughout the trial. He told the judge about how he never knew what was going on around him during the trial because he was just too drunk. And yet he was able to fake it so the judge never knew he was drunk. But he was.

"And I notice on the record," I began. "That there is not

one objection from you anywhere during that trial. Can you tell the court why you never objected to anything?"

"I never objected to anything because I never really heard anything the prosecutor had to say. I was in my own little world, my own bubble. I was thinking about my father the entire time, and, as I said before, I was drunk the entire time."

"And you did not put on any evidence on behalf of Jamel, right?"

"Yes, that's right. When it came time for me to put on evidence, I did not do it. I just wanted the trial to be over. It was the longest two weeks of my life. You have to understand, my father's death hit me really hard. We weren't close. Not at all. But I've gone to therapy on this and I realize my father's death hit me so hard because I never got closure with him on the issues I had with him over my life. When he died, I realized I never would. All I could think about all through that trial was about all the things I should've said to my father that I didn't. When it came time for me to put on evidence, I just wanted the whole thing over with."

At that point, I went through all the ways he could've presented a defense for Jamel. I talked about why he did not present pictures of the woman's house, why he never made the point to the jury that Jamel called 911, so why would he call 911 if he did it, and how would a street kid like Jamel could get onto the private property of a prominent actress like Felicity McDaniel. Most of all, he did not bother to call Jamel to the stand. Jamel would've been a very good witness. In fact, the whole story about Jamel finding Felicity after driving Uber never even made it to the jury. The prosecutor's story about Jamel wandering in off the street and raping Felicity was allowed to stand. In short, the prosecutor's entire case was allowed to stand, with no rebuttal. Of course the jury found Jamel guilty.

The entire hearing took the better part of the day, and although the prosecutor, Matthew, tried to cross-examine Jim, I knew by looking at the judge that he wasn't having it.

"Okay," Judge Warner said to Jim. Jim was still sitting on the stand, shaking. I had a feeling he wasn't shaking because he was scared, but that he probably was going through some kind of *delirium tremens*. Jim told me that he had not had a drink in three days so it looked like he was going through some kind of withdrawal. "Here's what I'm going to do. I'm going to reverse this case. I have reviewed the record prior to this hearing, of course. And I find ample evidence that if the counsel for Jamel Jackson was at all effective, Mr. Jackson would not have been convicted. This case has more holes in it than Butch and Sundance after the Bolivian army got through with them. More holes in it than Sonny Corleone at the Causeway. So I find both prongs are present in this case – the counsel was ineffective and the ineffectiveness of the counsel is what led to the conviction."

My heart started to pound. I didn't dare hope for such a good outcome, but here it was. I looked over at Jamel and squeezed his hand. He was crying.

The judge wasn't finished. "I find it particularly egregious that you, Mr. Howard, were so cynical as to strike every single member of the jury who is of color. I'm sure you didn't think you could get away with it, yet you did, just because Mr. Stack was completely checked out. However, I can't believe that you would even deign to violate this young man's constitutional rights in that manner. Even if you could get away with it, which you did, it doesn't make it right. Quite frankly, while I'm not going to question the motivations of the police force, I don't know why this young kid was even arrested for raping Ms. McDaniel, and I certainly don't know why he was even charged. It seems pretty clear from the record that the State of California's story that was given to the jury was, for lack of a better word, ridiculous. You presented evidence to the jury that a street kid could just wander onto the home of a prominent actress, scale her 10 foot tall wall surrounding her home, and then, once he's there, scale the 10 foot tall wall that led to her pool. Once again, if Mr. Stack was alive and well during the trial, he would never have let that pass. It seems pretty obvious to me from the record that the actual person who did this to Ms. McDaniel probably did it, and then called Uber, because he wanted somebody to take the fall. That was why young Mr. Jackson was able to get on the compound in the first place, because the real perpetrator left the gate open for him. And also apparently left the gate open to the pool. Now, that's just speculation on my part, and perhaps it's improper, but these are all questions in the case that should have been brought out by Mr. Stack, but weren't. And the reason why I am going into such length about what I think about this case is because I'm not going to remand it. If you want to retry this case, Mr. Howard, then you're going to have to refile it, and I hope you have a better basis for refiling the case the second time around. But I'm not going do your job for you. I'm hereby vacating the finding of Mr. Jackson's guilt."

Oh my God. This was going better than I ever hoped it would. When I took this case, I didn't dare believe it would go this well. But obviously the judge saw what any blind man could see —my client got a raw deal, he was not guilty, and the only reason why he was found guilty was because his attorney was asleep on the job.

"Thank you, Your Honor," I said.

"I'm not through. Mr. Stack, are you still drinking?"

Jim shrank down in his chair. "Your Honor, I have not had a drink in three days."

"That's not answering my question. You haven't had a drink in three days, so what? From what you told me on the stand, you are an alcoholic. I know something about alcoholics and they don't just quit drinking on their own. They need help. Are you going to Alcoholics Anonymous?"

"No, Your Honor, I'm not."

"And why aren't you going to AA?"

"Because, Your Honor, I don't believe in a higher power. If I don't believe in a higher power, how am I supposed to get anything out of AA?"

"You think that just because you are an atheist that AA won't work for you?"

"Yes. That's what I believe. I've looked online about AA, and I realize that most of the 12 steps have to do with turning my life over to God and I don't believe in God. So, I just don't think it will help me."

"How about rehab? Have you thought about that?"

Jim shook his head. "No. I do not have the money to go to rehab."

"So what's your plan? Because, until you get some kind of plan together, you're not going to be good for any client. You are a walking, talking, malpractice suit. I cannot, in good conscience, allow you to continue to practice law until you get your life together. Therefore, I'm going to have to report you to the bar on this case. The bar will force you to deal with your alcohol issues, one way or another. If you don't want to go to AA, and you can't afford to go to rehab, I don't know what to tell you. What I can tell you is that when the bar receives my complaint against you, they will hold a proceeding to disbar you. You have already been suspended for your alcohol issues, so you're skating on thin ice as it is. You've fallen through the ice this time. You might be able to save your license, but only if you stop drinking, one way or another."

"I understand."

"Do you? Do you understand? Because I'll be honest with you. I've never received a case this egregious in front of me in my entire life. I have never received a case where the attorney just did nothing throughout the trial. Did not object to anything, did not put on any evidence, let the prosecutor's story stand. Mr. Jackson would've been much better off if he would've represented himself. I don't want to ever see another case like this again."

At that, he banged his gavel and then stormed off the bench.

I looked over Jamel. He was still crying.

"Well, we did it," I said.

Matthew came over to me. "I wouldn't be so happy. Listen, the judge might have reversed the case, but I can file new charges against your client. And I plan to. I plan to. Because somebody will have to pay for what happened to that poor girl."

"Listen, you can do whatever you want, obviously," I said. "I can't stop you. However, if refile the case and you don't have any new evidence, just be prepared to fall flat on your face and be humiliated and embarrassed. Because I'll be taking Jamel's case. I'll be the one trying it. I won't let you get away with the same crap Mr. Stack let you get away with just because Mr. Stack was weak and drunk. . You'll be laughed out of court. You don't have anything and you know it. You just heard Judge Warner tell you that you had nothing."

I was infuriated. Here was his jackass, after the judge told him he didn't have anything, told him he was surprised the case was filed in the first place, and he was wanting to try the case again? And the reason why he wanted to try the case again was because nobody else was available for him to charge, and somebody would have to pay? I couldn't believe my ears.

"Listen," Matthew said. "And you listen good. I have a lot of pressure on me for this case. A lot of people coming down on me. I have to make sure it's wrapped up. If I have to try the case 100 times, and get reversed 100 times, so be it. But this case won't drag on and on forever without a suspect. You can't believe the kind of pressure coming down to make sure that somebody is put in prison for the rape of Felicity McDaniel. If you knew about that pressure, you would not question me."

I was about ready to explode at that point. "I *am* going to question you. I don't care what kind of pressure is on you to prosecute somebody who you know goddamn good and well is not good for the case. If you're willing to see him in prison for the rest of his life – that's just plain evil. It's not your life on the line here. You aren't the one who has a mother at home crying her eyes out every single night because she lost her one and only baby to the system. You aren't the one who will have to spend the rest of his life in prison for something somebody else clearly did. My client went through so much hardship these past few months. You would not believe the kinds of things he saw in prison. The things he's had to do. Do you know he was knifed in the lunch room? He was jumped by three men who wanted to get a piece of him, because his name is so notorious due to his association with this case. He was put into solitary, because he had to be put into protective custody, otherwise his life would continue to be in danger. If he would've died, would you want that on your head? Could you look his mother in the eye and tell her you did the right thing? You may look at Jamel and see a kid who is disposable. After all, he's poor. He's black. You probably think in your mind that a kid like Jamel could be thrown away, sacrificed so the real culprit can go free. I'm here to tell you that Jamel is not disposable. He is not a piece of trash. He is not your sacrifice. He is a living, breathing kid, with dreams just like everybody else. Hopes just like everybody else. He has a mother who loves him, just like everybody else. He deserves to have a life and you cannot take that from him. So, as you say, you can try the case 100 times and get reversed 100 times, and I will be on that case every goddamn time, holding you accountable."

I was shaking, I was so enraged.

I looked around and saw Aisha in the courtroom. She, like Jamel, was crying.

"I'm so sorry, Jamel, I wanted to be here for your hearing," Aisha was saying. "I wanted to be here, but I had to work late. Somebody called in, so I wasn't able to take off the afternoon. What did I miss?"

"Mama, I'm free to go. The judge, he reversed my conviction. I'm coming home, Mama."

I turned around and took one look at Matthew's face, and I knew he would be refiling the case immediately. He was just that kind of a jackass. He didn't care. All he knew was that his superiors were probably telling him that he better be pressing a case against somebody, and he obviously could not press the case against the person who did it. So he would have to keep coming after Jamel.

"This is true, Christian?" Aisha was asking. "Is my son really free to go?"

"Yes. That's true. However, I hate to say this, but your celebration might be short-lived. The prosecutor has already indicated that he wants to re-file the case. The appellate judge in this case said that he did not understand why the case was filed in the first place. Yet the prosecutor, Matthew Howard, is determined to get Jamel again. So I just wanted to warn you. You can go home and celebrate. Do what you can, enjoy your time together, because I would not be surprised if Jamel gets arrested again sometime within the next week."

"I don't understand. I didn't think you could be tried twice for the same thing," Aisha said, confused.

"Double jeopardy does not apply in a situation like this. Double jeopardy would only apply if he was found not guilty by a jury. He was not found not guilty - he was found guilty. All the judge here did was reverse the trial court and vacated your son's conviction. He did not remand it, which means he did not order the case to be retried. However, even if he reversed it, it does not mean the prosecutor will give up. He can refile the charges. And he's going to. So, this victory will probably be short-lived."

Aisha nodded. "I understand. But, like you say, for now, we're going to celebrate. Jamel, I got a little bit of money, let's go to Red Lobster. Your favorite place."

Jamel's entire face lit up. "Red Lobster? Are you sure you can afford that, mama?"

"I've been working a lot of overtime lately, so, yes, I can afford it. Don't you worry about that. You're my baby and you're out of prison. You might be out of prison just for a little while, hopefully not, but maybe. But, as long as you're free, you and I are going to make the most of it."

Jamel went over to her, hugged her and she hugged him back. She squeezed him hard, tears flowing down her face.

Then she turned to me. "I don't know how to thank you. You took this case for free. I told you when you came to my place that I thought God sent you to my life. Angels brought you down. I feel that way. It was divine intervention that you would come to us at this time. I can't help but think the same divine intervention will make sure my Jamel stays out of prison."

"Mr. Davis," Jamel said to me. "Would you like to come to dinner with us tonight?"

I wondered if Aisha had enough money to treat me. I knew she would want to, obviously, because I took her son's case. Red Lobster was not exactly expensive, but it was not exactly cheap, either. The last thing I wanted to do was take her last dime, because she was too proud to not treat me if I went to dinner with them.

"Yes, please, I should've asked you," Aisha said eagerly. "It's the least I can do."

I would have to find an excuse not to go. "I'd love to, but I have plans this evening. You guys have fun. I'll be in touch when I find out what's going to happen next."

"If you say so. I would love for you to come, though. Thank you again. I just don't know what I can do to thank you."

"Please. I'm doing it for selfish reasons. I'm doing it because it gives me a good feeling to help somebody who really needs justice. I read the case online, just like everybody else did, and I knew he had been done a great injustice. It just makes me feel good to make sure that I did my part to make sure the injustice did not stand."

She grasped my hand and clutched it for a second. I could see in her eyes deep gratitude, and Jamel's as well.

And then they were gone.

I hoped, and prayed, that this would be the last time I

would see Jamel. That would mean Jamel went on with his life without getting charged again.

But I knew that was unlikely to happen. I knew it just by looking at that smug Matthew Howard's face.

I was just going to have to brace myself for the inevitable.

Chapter Thirteen

MATTHEW HOWARD

MATTHEW HOWARD SAT in his office, knowing what he had to do. It wasn't that he enjoyed putting an innocent man through the wringer. No, it wasn't that. It was that he understood one thing – he would have to button up the case of the rape of Felicity McDaniel, and he would have to do it without implicating the person who really was responsible. And, while he didn't enjoy putting Jamel into jail again, which was where Jamel would go once he refiled the case, because he knew Jamel did not have money for bail, he also did not mind putting him back behind bars. Jamel was a street punk, a thug, and they were all alike, anyhow. Not one of the dark-skinned guys that he prosecuted from the streets were innocent, not really. Yeah, maybe some of them were innocent of the crime he charged them with, but he knew that every one of them was guilty of something else, something they were not caught for. He had no doubt Jamel was the same. He knew the type - the gang bangers, the drug dealers, the people who preyed on children, getting them hooked on drugs. They were all packing, ready to use their guns on each other at any moment. There was a part of him that just wanted them to finish the job on each other and not prosecute people caught with illegal weapons, dealing drugs, or just possessing drugs. If he didn't do his job, putting those people into jail and prison, they could just die off by killing each other. And the world would be a better place.

So no, he did not feel a tinge of guilt about refiling the case against Jamel. After all, if he did not put Jamel away for this, it would only be a matter of time before he would be putting him away for something. Might as well just save time and get the real perpetrator off the hook at the same time. Everybody wins.

He got a phone call. It was his boss. His superior. He would have to answer for the fact that Jamel was currently out and free as a bird. He would get yelled at and he knew it. He was just going to have to suck it up.

"I need to see you in my office, right now."

His boss, Michael Christie, did not sound happy in the least. Of course he didn't. Matthew lost the case. It was an imperative that he not lose the case, but, at the same time, he kind of knew going in that he was a dead man walking. But what did they expect? They were the ones who made sure the case was assigned to a drunk. They were gambling that once Jamel went down, he would stay there, because nobody would bother to take his case. They certainly were not banking on some do-gooder deciding to take Jamel's case for free. Christian Davis spoiled everybody's plans and he would have to pay for it. Later. For now, Matthew was just going to have to get his ass chewed. As much as he hated it, he knew it was coming, so he might as well just face the music. Pay the piper. Get it over and done.

He reluctantly went down to Michael's office. He felt like a dog about to be punished. A prisoner about to be taken to the execution.

"I hear you lost in court yesterday," Michael said. "What the hell happened?"

"What do you think happened? Listen, what happened yesterday was because we were far too cute by half. What did you think would happen when we got a guy like Jim Stack defending Jamel? Did you think a writ of *habeas corpus* wouldn't be given when a guy like Jim was defending Jamel? Did you actually think a case like that would not be reversed?"

"I know what you're saying, but we were supposed to have taken care of Christian before the hearing. Why didn't that happen?"

Matthew knew what Michael was saying, and he also knew that what Michael wanted was not going to happen. At least it was not going to happen on Matthew's watch.

"Listen, I did what I could. I sent Felicity over to talk to him and it didn't do any good. Felicity told him about the stakes, and he still went ahead."

"Well, what are we going to do now?"

"I'm going to refile it, of course."

Michael shook his head. "And then what? We have a flimsy case, at best, and we had the best chance possible when we had that nigger in jail. We were home free and you fucked it up. Now I want to know what you're going to do about the next step. I mean, Jamel will get a new trial, obviously. We can't necessarily count on a wastoid like Jim Stack taking his case. We can't count on that at all. Probably that Christian, that damn do-gooder social justice warrior Christian, he'll probably be on the case again. He'll do all the investigation Jim didn't do. He'll do all the cross-examination Jim didn't do. He'll make sure there are people of color on the jury. And he'll put on an active defense. He'll do everything Jim was supposed to have done if he was a halfway decent attorney and he's going to win the case. You're just going to have to figure out some way to get rid of Christian, once and for all."

"Listen, I hate to tell you this, but Jamel is going to be eligible for another public defender if I refile the case. So even if Christian does not take the case, he's going to get somebody else to take it. I mean, we can't force that office to hire another loser like Jim Stack, can we?"

"We didn't force nobody. We simply threatened to expose the dirty little secrets of the lead public defender and he saw the light in hiring that guy. That's all we did. There was no forcing involved. And I don't want to hear you say there was."

Matthew supposed that was true but it was a distinction without a difference. The lead public defender, Robert Donahue, was having an affair and his wife was very wealthy. Michael found out Robert had a very strict no-adultery clause in the prenuptial agreement that he signed with his millionaire heiress wife, Marissa, and if Marissa ever got ahold of the pictures that Michael's private investigator took of Robert and the man he was having an affair with, he would be divorced and cut off without a penny. Yes, he was having an affair with a man. That was another dirty secret he was dying to keep hidden from his wife and from everybody else.

Robert, despite the fact that he was doing God's work, or that's what he would tell everybody, for not a ton of money, really did have some pretty champagne tastes with his beer bottle pocket. He really enjoyed going out on

Marissa's yacht and he could not do without the long vacations taken at her sun-soaked beach house in Crete. He was surprised about how much he had come to rely on his wife's money, so when it was threatened that he would be cut off, he did whatever he could to make sure that did not happen. And that included hiring Jim Stack, a man nobody else would touch. He hired him mainly to try this particular case, but he also knew Jim would come in handy in other cases where things were as delicate as they were with this one. He knew Jamel was a fall guy and he knew there would be other fall guys in the future. The monster who raped Felicity McDaniel slipped up when he raped her, because usually he raped people who did not matter in society, and Robert knew he would slip up again in the future. That would mean other fall guys for his crimes. That would mean other defense attorneys were going to have to completely sleepwalk through cases. That was why he wanted Jim on the staff, so he was very disappointed when Jim decided to quit and go into private practice. Jim was very useful to him. He was just going to have to find someone else like him. Some other stooge who lived in a bottle and could be counted on to blow off any case he got.

"I know you don't want to use the term force when we talk about the public defender's office hiring Jim Stack, but that's really what it was," Matthew told his boss, stating the brutally obvious.

Michael drummed his fingers on the desk. "Okay, here's what we're going to do. We are going to take care of Christian, one way or another. He cannot be the trial attorney for Jamel. Jamel has to stay in prison. And you know why."

Of course Matthew knew why. They had no other suspects for the case, and, once the case went cold, the police were going to start investigating again to try to find out who really did it, and then their investigation would probably lead them to the real culprit.

And that certainly could not happen.

Chapter Fourteen

CHRISTIAN

THAT NIGHT, after Jamel was freed, I went back to my home in San Diego and went for my nightly run along the Embarcadero. When I was home, I took the same route, every single day, because I'd mapped it out on my GPS, and I knew that it was exactly 6 miles. I would start out on the Embarcadero, wind my way up through Little Italy, and on up through Baker's Hill, and would end up in the Hillcrest area, before running back. It was something I did all the time to clear my head and also because I really loved the old neighborhoods between my condo and the Hillcrest area. Some of the houses in the Baker's Hill area were built around the turn-of-the-century and I always tried to imagine what they looked like back then and what the area itself looked like. San Diego was a fairly new city, when you compared it to some of the cities in the Midwest and back East, so there weren't a lot of historical neighborhoods, but Baker's Hill was one of them.

As I ran, I thought about what had happened that day. I was excited because Jamel's case turned out better than I could have ever dreamed, but at the same time, I was very apprehensive. There was something nagging at me. It wasn't just the fact that I knew for a fact that Jamel was still imperiled. It was something else. It was the words that Felicity said to me when she came to my office. The warning. What did she mean?

I knew what she meant. I didn't really want to look at it, but I knew what she meant. She meant that if I pursued Jamel's case, I would be putting myself into danger. And if there was somebody, or something, that I really cared about, like children, I would've played along. If I had kids, and they were threatened, I would've done what Felicity had asked. But it was only my own self being threatened. I could take care of myself. I was a grown-ass man. Besides, nobody had ever truly threatened me before. I've had death threats before, just like most defense attorneys do sooner or later. Kooks were legion and so were trolls. I couldn't get scared every time a troll threatened me, otherwise I would never leave the house.

I ran up the sidewalk and passed the enormous three-story homes built with brick, with their wraparound porches and turrets, and then proceeded up the hill towards Hillcrest. Hillcrest was known as the gay area of town, where the annual pride parade snaked, with its wide array of drag queens with three-foot tall wigs, along with an endless supply of people trying to sell insurance behind a banner. I used to go to the parades, just because I found them entertaining, but after a little while, they got pretty boring. There were only so many boring banners with boring people marching that one could watch without the entire thing becoming extremely uninteresting. The drag queen floats, unfortunately, were few and far between, so I just stopped going to the parade. But I still enjoyed the Hillcrest area, mainly because some of the best restaurants in town were in this area, along with a Whole Foods, one of only three in San Diego County. I really liked Whole Foods, in spite of the inflated prices on things, because nobody could beat their selection of organic groceries. Sometimes when I made my run up to Hillcrest, I would carry a backpack with me and haul some grass-fed steaks and wild-caught King Salmon home.

I ran up the street, passing by a large park that had a building in the middle advertising bridge games, as the sun was going down. From the corner of my eye, I saw a guy coming up on my right, and he was running very fast. I got further to the left of the sidewalk to let him pass, thinking how rude it was that he was passing me on the right, instead of on the left, when I tripped and fell on the sidewalk.

I felt a metal object bash against the back of my head.

And that's the last thing I remembered.

Chapter Fifteen

CHRISTIAN

I WOKE up in the hospital, and saw that I was hooked up to a machine. I had no idea how I got there or why I was there. It seemed I had been going on my usual run, and then – what happened?

I looked to my left and saw Avery sleeping in a chair. "You're awake!" she said excitedly. "Let me go get the doctor."

What was she talking about? Why was she so excited about my being awake?

A doctor came in and immediately put a flashlight in my eyes. I tried not to blink, but it was very difficult. "How are you feeling?" he asked as he took my pulse.

"Okay, I guess. My head hurts. Why?"

"You've been in a medically induced coma for the past two weeks. When you were brought in, your brain was dangerously swelling. We've had to put you into a medically induced coma until the swelling went down. I'm going to send you down to have some tests done to make sure the swelling has decreased enough that you are no longer in danger. That said, the last time we took a CAT scan, your brain swelling had significantly reduced, which is why we brought you out of your coma. When you're feeling up to it, we would like to call the police so you can give a report as to how you ended up with such a traumatic brain injury."

I didn't know what he was talking about. I only knew my head hurt. Throbbed. I looked over at Avery, who looked like she had been sleeping in her clothes for the past three days, and I had a question in my eyes.

I didn't have to even verbalize a question, however.

"They found you laying on the sidewalk next to the San Diego Bridge Academy." This was the building in the park where I ran by almost every evening. "Somebody apparently hit you on the back of your head and ran off. Do you know who would do that to you? They found your wallet on you, so obviously this was not a robbery incident. Your wallet had $200 in it and all your credit cards. The police are dumbfounded as to who would've smashed you like that, and then just ran off, without asking for anything. So maybe you can talk to the cops and give them some ideas."

I blinked. "Jamel. What about Jamel?"

"Matthew Howard refiled the rape case against him. That same rape case he was imprisoned for before. He's already had his arraignment. He's back in jail. Don't worry, he has a new attorney. It's a guy by the name of Dallas Wilcox. He's in private practice. He took the case for free. So, don't worry, Jamel is in good hands."

"No. No he is not in good hands. What do you know about this Dallas Wilcox?"

"Just that he's a criminal defense attorney. I admit, he's not very well known in the Los Angeles bar, because he's new to the area. Why are you getting so upset?"

"I'm upset because I think this Dallas Wilcox person is

on Jamel's case because he's probably being paid off. I need to do some background information on him, find out what his deal is. I'll bet if I get into it, I'm going to find financial problems galore, and probably also find a very large amount of money transferred into his account. Or maybe I'll find he's got some kind of kiddie porn on his computer, or something of the sort. He's either being bribed or blackmailed, but what I can tell you is that he's going to throw this case. He's going to throw it while not being as obvious about it as Jim Stack was."

"Don't worry about that. The prosecutor's office has already come up with a plea agreement, and I've talked to Jamel about it, and I think he's going to take it. He told me they're offering him the chance to plead down to an assault in the 1st°, 10 years in prison. Dallas is really pressing Jamel to take this plea agreement, because, after all, Jamel was already convicted for this rape once before and he'll probably be convicted again. He was facing life in prison for that rape. Jamel thinks it's an okay deal, considering that 10 years is obviously a lot less than life. He's 18 years old. He'll be out before he's 30."

"Jamel told you about this and what did you say?"

"What could I say? I had to give him my opinion as a lawyer. I told him all the pros and cons, and you have to admit, taking this case to trial would be risky, to say the very least. He was already convicted once on this charge. So I talked to Jamel and I told him that while the appellate judge didn't believe there was enough evidence for him to have been convicted, he would have to roll the dice for a second time if he didn't take this plea agreement, and there was a chance the jury would find the evidence compelling enough to put him into prison again. I told him that outcome probably would not happen, because the appellate judge thought the evidence is lacking, but that there was a chance it could happen and this plea agreement was a bird in his hand and it was worth two in the bush. He asked what that meant, and I told him that it was a saying that something you have in your hand is worth two of something you don't have, but hope to."

I suddenly felt a sense of panic. "When is his plea agreement scheduled?"

"It's scheduled for tomorrow at 1:30. Why do you ask that question?"

"Because he didn't do it. How is he going to do a plea agreement if he can't make a factual basis?"

"Dallas said that he's doing an Alford Plea." An Alford Plea was a plea agreement where the defendant admitted there was enough evidence against him to convict in a court of law but that he was not going to admit to having done it.

"You have to stop this. You have to. If he pleads guilty, he won't be coming back. There will be no writ of *habeas corpus*, no appeal, if he pleads guilty. Goddammit, that's their new trick. Try to make him believe he's taking a great deal so they can plead him guilty and foreclose his right to appeal. Why didn't you try to talk him out of this?"

"For the same reason I try to get my clients to take a plea agreement when they're facing life in prison. Somebody comes at you with a 10 year offer to a lesser charge and you have to think twice about passing that up. You have to think about what would happen at trial, and the possibility you're going to be facing a much stiffer sentence if you're found guilty by the jury. I know I don't have to tell you this. It's criminal defense 101. You just have to look at the odds and roll the dice, or not. In this case, Jamel decided not to roll the dice. As I said, he's looking at the fact that he's going to be getting out of prison before he is 30 years old, in time to have a life, as opposed to never getting out of prison if he's convicted."

"But, Avery, why would you advise him to take this plea agreement, when you read the transcripts for the appellate judge and you saw the appellate judge said there was not enough evidence to convict him? The appellate judge would know better than anybody else what quality of evidence is sufficient to convict somebody. And he stated on the record there was not enough to charge him with the crime, let alone convict him. Why couldn't you go with that?"

"Because, the prosecutor has new evidence and it's enough to convict him this time."

"What's that supposed to mean? What does he have that he didn't have before?""

"The victim, Felicity McDaniel. She's offered to testify and she's offered to testify that Jamel was the person who raped her."

Chapter Sixteen

CHRISTIAN

"FELICITY MCDANIEL." I looked at the ceiling and realized my blood pressure was going dangerously high at that point. I could see the monitor leaping up, showing my blood pressure at that moment was 170/100. I took a deep breath and tried to calm down and saw my blood pressure gradually receding.

I couldn't believe Felicity McDaniel would lie like that.

"Avery, don't you think it's a little bit odd that she told the cops all along that she had no idea who raped her, and now, suddenly, she remembered?"

"Yes, I do believe that's odd. However, she's willing to testify he raped her. Dallas told me she was put under hypnosis and she clearly remembered he did that to her. So she's going to court to testify against him. Once Jamel found that out, he knew he would have to take this offer."

I would have get out of the hospital before 1:30 tomorrow. "Listen, I'm checking myself out of this hospital. Today. There's no way I can allow that kid to throw away his life like this. He didn't do it. Felicity herself told me he didn't do it. She told me he had to pay for raping her all the same, even though he's innocent and he saved her life. So I can tell you that she's being pressured by somebody to testify against him, and I need to find out who that person is. If I had to hazard a guess, I would say the same person who pressured her to testify against Jamel is the one who put that mugger up to hitting me on that sidewalk. Somebody is pulling everybody strings on this and I need to find out who it is. So I need to get out of this hospital today."

"You can't get out of the hospital until the doctor says you can. You've been in a medically-induced coma for the past two weeks. You can't just up and leave. You have an IV in your arm. What are you going to do, just take it out?"

"If I have to. All I know is that I need to get out of this hospital to talk to Jamel in jail. I need to tell him the truth about Felicity. About how she came to see me and told me she remembered who did this to her and it wasn't him. And I need to make sure this Dallas Wilcox person gets off of his case immediately so I can get on it."

"You need to slow your roll. You can't leave until the doctor clears you to leave. Now sit back and relax. When the doctor says you can leave, you will leave. But not before that."

"Okay then. You need to go down and talk to Jamel and tell him to fire that Dallas Wilcox, yesterday. Dallas Wilcox does not have Jamel's best interest at heart, and, quite frankly, I'm thinking the same thing about you. You need to fix this. I can't fix this, not from a hospital bed, but you can."

"What are you talking about? Do you really want him to spend the rest of his life in prison? Do you? I know you say Felicity came to see you and admitted to you privately that she knew Jamel did not attack her, but what kind of evidence is that? It's he said, she said, and the woman is an actress. She'll be able to give an Academy Award-winning performance on the stand and the jury will eat it up. She's going to lie on the stand and how can you stop her? If you can't stop her from lying on the stand, it's bye-bye Birdie for Jamel. He will die in prison. This way, he goes into prison not as a rapist, but as a guy who committed an assault. You know as well as I do that in the prison hierarchy, the guys who committed assaults are much higher on the totem pole than guys who committed rapes. You know he's going to have a much easier time going into prison without a rape conviction on his record. And, like I said, he'll be out before he's 30. He'll have his chance to set things straight. He'll have his chance to live his life. He'll have all the chances you wanted for him, to find a woman and get married, have kids, have a career, all of that. He doesn't take this deal, and Felicity testifies against him in court, and he will have nothing. You just have to think of it from that angle."

"Do what you can to at least postpone it. I really need to find the real culprit in this situation and I need to do what I can to make sure he stops pulling everybody's strings. I need that chance."

"I'll do what I can, but I don't think it'll work. Dallas told me the prosecutor's offer was only good for 24 hours. I don't think the prosecutor's office will go along with a continuance of the case without withdrawing the offer. You know the prosecutor's office has all the leverage here, with Felicity being willing to testify and all. I'm sorry, but I just don't think a continuance is possible without risking losing that offer."

I suddenly felt hopeless. There I was, lying supine in my hospital bed, while Jamel was getting ready to make the biggest mistake of his life. Or maybe not taking the plea would've been a bigger mistake? I knew it was wrong. I knew Jamel was innocent, factually innocent. The victim told me so. And yet he was set to spend 10 years of his life behind bars, probably at a maximum security prison, for something he did not do.

But maybe Avery was right. It would be an enormous risk to take Jamel's case to trial again, even if I was the one trying it. Avery was correct that Felicity McDaniel was known to be a very good actress. She had been nominated for several Golden Globes, several Emmys, and even the Academy Award, twice. She would be able to put on a show for the jury, and if she did put on a show for the jury, that would be all she wrote. Jamel would be spending the rest of his life behind bars.

Goddammit. Jamel was put into an impossible situation. I wanted so badly to get out of the hospital and talk him out of it, but what if I talked him out of it, and he ended up behind bars for life? Would I be able to live with myself? Would I be able to look at myself in the mirror, knowing that I was responsible for the absolute destruction of a boy's life?

I looked over at Avery. I suddenly did not want her in the hospital room anymore. I needed to be alone with my thoughts. I needed to have some time to contemplate this situation and really think about how to tackle it. I needed to come up with a plan before 1:30 tomorrow. I needed to figure out a way to get out of the hospital so that I could put the plan, whatever it happened to be, into action.

"Avery, I'm really tired. I'm sorry, but I'm going to have to ask you to come back at a different time." I closed my eyes so she could get the hint.

"Christian, I know what you're going to try to do and I don't think you should. I don't think there is much we can do before Jamel's guilty plea tomorrow. I know your brain is turning, but I've thought about this too, eight ways to Sunday, and I really believe Jamel is doing the right thing. But I'll leave, since you want me to. But, I'm just telling you, don't interfere."

"Avery, you of all people should not be encouraging an innocent man to go to prison. And that's all I have to say."

"Well, that was hitting below the belt. I'll come back and check on you later." And, at that, Avery was gone.

Chapter Seventeen

CHRISTIAN

AFTER AVERY LEFT, I lay in my hospital bed, just stewing. I was feeling nauseated, even though I knew the problem that landed me in the hospital bed was a head injury. The nausea came from the terrible pit I had in my stomach, the burning, aching, dark sensation that the Jamel Jackson case had gone horribly awry. I didn't like the helpless feeling, but I knew I had to do something.

My cell phone was in the nightstand next to me so I dialed Regina's number. She answered on the second ring.

"Hey Christian, what's shaking?"

"How is your investigation going for the Jamel Jackson case?" I asked her.

"He has a new attorney, so I haven't been working the case for the past couple of weeks. By the way, how are you feeling?"

"I'm feeling fine. I need to get out of this bed. Listen, I need for you to get back on the case. I know, I know, Jamel has a new lawyer and you'll be stepping on his toes. Don't worry about that, just do it on the down low. I need to have something done by 1:30 tomorrow. Something, anything, that I can sink my teeth into. I also need for you to create some kind of a distraction for a lawyer by the name of Dallas Wilcox. Can you do that ?"

"What kind of a distraction do you want me to create for Dallas Wilcox? And who is Dallas Wilcox?"

"Dallas Wilcox is Jamel's new attorney. I'll give you his address and phone number. Are you ready?"

I gave her the phone number and she wrote it down.

"Okay, I'll ask you again. What kind of distraction do you want me to use with Dallas Wilcox?" Regina asked.

"Go over there and see him. Make an appointment. And wear something low-cut."

I could almost hear Regina rolling her eyes after I told her to see him while wearing something low-cut. "Oh, this again. I'm supposed to use my looks to manipulate a dude. You know, it's pretty amazing that that works. You just go in there, flash a little breast, and you suddenly got a guy eating out of your hands. Why is it so easy to get things from men?"

"Because men think with their dicks," I said. "Listen, I don't like asking you to do this, because I know you and Aidan are trying to work things out. I know you just started dating him. Believe me, I would not ask you to do this if it was not an emergency. However, it is an emergency. Like a four alarm fire at this point. So I really need for you to use all of your feminine charms to try to not only convince this guy to ask for a continuance on Jamel's plea court appearance tomorrow, but also try to extract some information from him. I have a feeling he knows exactly what's going on in this case. If my hunch is correct, the puppet-master in all of this probably decided not to go with a clueless stooge to represent Jamel, but, rather, went with a guy who's in on the game. If my hunch is right and you can get some information out of him, that will do wonders for this case. It'll crack it. Of course, getting the information will one thing. Proving it is going to be quite another."

Regina groaned. "Okay, I'll do what I can. I'll let you know what happens."

Chapter Eighteen

REGINA

REGINA CURSED as she put on her special dress that always worked to get what she wanted. It was a black number, tight, clingy, and plunging, which showed off her impressive rack. It was also super short, so she was able to show off her legs, which were tight and toned from running and squatting. She didn't normally wear makeup, it clogged her pores, but she decided to put on some eyeliner, mascara, lipstick, and a light foundation.

She really did not want to do this. However she also knew Jamel was facing 10 years in prison, so she knew it was important to slow this whole thing down. When Avery told her about Jamel agreeing to take a plea agreement, the first thing she thought was, why? Yeah, she found out the victim would testify against Jamel in court. That was a game-changer. But she didn't like the feeling that this whole thing would be over before anybody had a chance to do some real investigation.

But Christian was in the hospital, and, at first, nobody knew if he would make it out of there in one piece. His injury was so severe that he had to be put into a medically-induced coma so that his brain could heal. But anytime you are in a coma, medically induced or no, there was always a risk you're not going to come out of it, and if you do, you might be a vegetable. Fortunately, Christian seemed to be no worse for the wear. Regina had just talked to him and he seemed as sharp as ever. That was obviously a relief. But now that he was awake, he apparently would try to go balls to the wall for Jamel. The only way he could do that was for Regina to work her magic on Dallas Wilcox. So it was what it was. She was just going to have to do what she had done on many previous occasions – use her face and body to get somebody to do something they wouldn't ordinarily do.

Of course, there was a big chance this would not work. For one thing, Regina might not be Dallas' type. She knew there were plenty of men who loved her tough-chick look – the tattoo sleeve, the solid muscles in her arms and legs, her overall attitude that screamed that she was a woman not to be messed with. But there were also plenty of men who preferred a more demure type of woman. For these men, Regina's body was a turnoff, even if they usually did appreciate her rack, which was always obvious by their stares. A lot of men preferred somebody thinner, blonder, paler, and quieter. If this guy liked women who looked like they could kick some ass, then he would like her. But if this guy preferred a cookie-cutter Barbie doll type, he wouldn't be manipulated by her. So she just had to hope he was in the category of somebody who liked the way that she looked. And even if a guy did not appreciate her body, they usually appreciated her face. That was the one constant. And she knew that her combination of high cheekbones, green eyes, full pouty lips, and perfectly symmetrical features, all set against her olive skin, along with her mane of thick dark hair, got most men to notice her.

She got to his office, which was quite a drive from San Diego, as it was in Studio City, and walked in. This guy seemed like he was doing okay, judging by his office. At least, this office looked more officey than the one the last attorney apparently worked in, according to Christian's description of Jim Stack's office suite. Dallas' office was a smallish office, with a small waiting room that sported hardwood floors, two leather couches and a coffee table. There was art on the walls and some classical music piped in through an overhead speaker. Regina realized this was not necessarily a suite so much as it was a waiting room and one office. In that one office, she could see through the window that a guy was talking on the phone. She had to assume the guy who was talking on the phone was Dallas.

She sat down on the couch and flipped through some magazines, and tried hard to hear what Dallas was talking about. He did not see her walk in, as his back was to the window when she walked in, and now she was sitting down, out of eye view. So, if the guy started talking loudly, she would be able to pick out snippets of what he was saying.

About five minutes into his phone conversation, she did hear him get loud.

And what she heard was dynamite.

Chapter Nineteen

CHRISTIAN

"I KNOW WHAT YOU'RE SAYING," Dallas was shouting into the phone. "And I'm going to get it done. You don't have to yell at me."

As Regina casually flipped through a magazine, she was intensely curious about what Dallas had to get done. She listened some more.

"I told you, Jamel is going to plead guilty tomorrow, and that's going to be that. The blood lust will be satisfied and Tim will be satisfied as well."

Tim. He was definitely talking about Jamel's case, but who was Tim? And why did he have to be satisfied?

"I know, I know. I know that if this whole thing goes south, you're not going to be able to retire early. You've told me that 100 times. You don't have to tell me again."

He paused for less than a minute, before he shouted again. "Yes, I know. I know the vice president wants to become president in four years or so and I know he can't do it if everybody knows what a monster his son is. If you ask me, maybe that mother-fucker should have spent a little more time tending to his own son, instead of preaching to everybody about what they're doing wrong. If there's one thing I hate, it's a hypocrite. I mean, all he has been able to talk about over his career is family values. He's always going on and on about how our society has become so coarse and how we all need to pray every day and put God back into the public square, and ban pornography, while he's quietly paying off people to make sure his violent rapist son can keep on doing what he's doing. I mean, how many people over the years have ended up near death because of that monster? And yes, I do consider hookers and homeless women to be people too. I know Tim thinks they are disposable, which I think is despicable."

Tim. Regina had a hard time wrapping her head around the fact that Dallas was talking about Timothy Harrison, the current vice president of the United States. But, then again, the description of a holy roller who wanted a theocratic government, who wanted to send our society back to the 1950s, where minorities, gays and women "knew their place," sounded like him. And Regina had to admit that from what she knew about this guy, he probably would be the type to protect his son from paying for his crimes, even if it meant an innocent black boy would pay instead. *Especially* if it meant an innocent black boy would pay. That was how guys like Timothy rolled – certain people were entitled to citizenship in the United States, and all that citizenship entailed and conferred, while others were considered to be less-than in some way. Regina, as a former sex worker, would definitely fall into the less-than category in Timothy's eyes.

So would Jamel.

Dallas appeared to know that what he was doing was wrong with Jamel, so Regina wondered what was in it for him. Why was he selling Jamel down the river? Why did he decide to take this case?

She found out soon enough.

"I know, I know, I have to get this done. I know that if I don't, those mobsters will be on my doorstep. Believe me, I know it's life or death for me to get this done. But I just wish I knew a different way of doing it."

Regina smiled. She wondered how much money Dallas owed to the mobsters and why he owed the money. Regina knew plenty of people in the Eastern European mobs that ran Southern California and she knew they did not fuck around. So everything was becoming clear. This guy took the case for the money. She listened closely to see if the money he owed was a huge amount of money or a relatively small amount. $25,000 or less, would be, in Regina's eyes, a doable amount. Anything more than that, and she would not be able to work with it.

"You know what's so crazy," Dallas was saying. "I only owe those goons $5,000. And here I am, selling my soul, because I don't know what else to do to get them off my back. They need the money tomorrow, so I have to do what I know is wrong so I can live another day. I'm exactly the person I never wanted to be." He paused for a few minutes. "I know, I'm getting into gamblers anonymous today. In the meantime, if I want to live out the week, I gotta get this done."

Regina quietly slipped out the front door. She knew the conversation was winding down and if he decided to leave his office and see her sitting there, she might be in trouble. But, if she simply left, while he was not watching her leave, she could come back in an hour or so and do her thing. And he would never know she was there for that conversation.

So when he turned his back to her again, she walked out the front door.

The first thing she did was head over to the beach. She drove down Sunset Boulevard to the Santa Monica pier, parked her car, and headed down to the area were all the vendors were. There was something about the carnival atmosphere of the pier that made her believe that she could get lost in the crowd, even if she was dressed like a hoochie mama. She took off her shoes and dangled them from her fingers and went up to a guy selling tacos and ordered two of them. Then she went down to the sand and sat down, eating her tacos while she thought about her next move.

So now she knew the truth – the vice president was behind all of it. His son was the real culprit. Now that she knew that, what next? How could she possibly prove any of it? And apparently everybody was so afraid and intimidated by him that they all were going with the nefarious plan to sell Jamel down the river for Vice-President Harrison's son's crimes. How was she going to circumvent the blockade?

She didn't know. She did know that she had to stop the proceedings. Jamel couldn't plead guilty.

By hook or by crook, she would make sure he didn't.

Chapter Twenty

REGINA

REGINA WENT BACK TO DALLAS' office a couple of hours later. This time, she actually made her presence known to Dallas as he sat in his office. She went over to his door, which was half-cracked, and knocked lightly on it. Dallas looked up at her, and she could see, by the expression on his face, that he was a man who found her attractive. His entire face lit up, although he tried to hide it.

He cleared his throat and nervously took some files that were on his desk and put them on the floor next to him. "Hello, can I help you?" he asked.

"Yes, I think you can," Regina said. "You're the lawyer for Jamel Jackson, aren't you?"

He looked down at the desk and cleared his throat again. "If you can call it that," he said. "Who's asking?"

"Well," Regina began. She had actually cleared a plan with Christian before she came to this office, and she hoped against hope it would work. "I was wondering if you would be willing to withdraw from his case. I work for an attorney, Christian Davis, who really wants on that case. You see, he was the attorney for Mr. Jackson for Mr. Jackson's appellate trial. He managed to get Mr. Jackson out on a writ, and, well, he feels very close to him."

Dallas shook his head. "Believe me, I wish that I weren't involved in that mess. But I am."

"Would you like to do some work for Mr. Davis? He would be willing to pay you an advance of $5,000 if you would be willing to work for him." Regina raised an eyebrow and leaned forward, making sure Dallas got a good look down her dress. "And I work for him, too. You and I would be working together."

Dallas' face got red and he nervously ran his fingers through his thick curly hair. "What, what, what would I be doing for, uh, what did you say his name was?" he asked while he stared at Regina's cleavage.

"Christian Davis. He really wants Jamel's case, so he's essentially willing to buy it off from you. Of course, you would have to earn the $5,000 by doing lawyer work for him, but he can pay you that money up front. Like, today. An automatic transfer to your PayPal. What do you say?"

Dallas didn't say anything for several seconds. He was too mesmerized by Regina's breasts. Regina rolled her eyes, making sure Dallas didn't catch her doing that, but she didn't move a muscle. She remained leaning over the desk, giving Dallas the best possible look at her marvelous rack.

"An automatic transfer to PayPal?" he finally said. "Uh, what do I have to do for him, again?"

"You have to simply get off Jamel's case. Withdraw from it today. Then you have to sign a contract for services for Christian. He needs somebody to help him prepare for Jamel's trial, ironically, and he figured you would be perfect for that job because you know so much about it. And, as I say, if you do this, you'll be $5,000 richer by the end of today. So are you game for that or not?"

Dallas finally leaned back and appeared to contemplate the offer for a few minutes. Regina knew he would take it, though. He only took the Jamel case because somebody, probably the bastard VP himself, paid him to take that case, or, more likely, promised to pay him after he got the plea agreement settled. He was desperate for some quick cash to pay off some mobster goons and he didn't like knowing that he was sending an innocent kid to prison to get that money. As far as Regina was concerned, his taking her offer was a no-brainer.

He finally looked up at the ceiling. "Oh, boy," he began. "If I get off that case, somebody is going to be pissed. To say the very least. But your offer is tempting. I don't want to plead that kid guilty."

"Because you know he didn't do it?" Regina asked innocently.

"Well, I don't that for sure," he said. "But-"

Regina leaned forward again. "Are you positive you don't know that for sure?"

Dallas licked his lips, which grossed Regina out, but she tried hard not to show it. "Oh, God, I do know he didn't do it. But I can't tell you who did. Jesus Christ, if I did that, I would really be signing my own death warrant. But, no, he didn't do it."

"Then it's good that you won't be pleading him guilty, then, isn't it?"

"I never agreed to what you're proposing. I have to think about things."

"What do you need to think about?" Regina asked. "You won't be sending an innocent kid to prison and you also will be getting a lot of money up front. You'll be working to free that kid instead of condemning him. Everybody wins. Right?"

Dallas looked at Regina, obviously trying to decide if he should tell her more. "I wish it were that simple. As it is, I'm into this pretty deep. I know somebody will have my balls in a jar if I do what you're asking me to do. It won't be pretty."

"What if I told you that I know who raped Felicity McDaniel," Regina asked. "And I have a plan to bring him down?"

Dallas cocked his head and laughed. "Oh, you know who raped her, do you? Tell me."

"His name is Noel Harrison. He's the son of the current vice-president." Regina folded her arms in front of her and stared at Dallas. She watched as his face turned a million shades of pink and red and his bony fingers nervously ran through his thick curly hair.

"Why do you think he did it?" Dallas asked. "You know that guy runs Hollywood. He's like one of the biggest movie producers in town. Why would he do something like that?"

Watching his reaction, Regina knew she had pinpointed exactly who was responsible for the rape of Felicity McDaniel. She had a one in three chance of getting it right, because VP Harrison had three sons. She did some quick research on all three of the sons and found out that one of them, Rory, was a hipster surfer who lived in the valley, and, as far as Regina was able to tell, he didn't do much except for live off his daddy's trust fund. Regina mentally ruled him out, mainly because she had an image of him as being a pot-head, and all the potheads she had ever known were far from violent. She knew she was stereotyping, but she had to narrow down the choices somehow.

The other son's name was Max. He was more interesting to Regina, because he was an investment banker on Wall Street. When Regina found that out, she kept it in mind, because, stereotyping again, she had an image of a high-strung guy who was a Type A and was probably a misogynist. That fit the profile of all the investment bankers she had ever known and she had actually known quite a few investment bankers in her life, mainly from her days of being a stripper and a sex worker. Then again, she thought that maybe the investment bankers she knew self-selected, as most investment bankers did not necessarily visit hookers, and the ones that did were probably different from the ones that did not.

Still, she did not have a very good view of Wall Street bankers.

So she definitely wanted to keep Max in mind. However, when she hit upon Noel, she thought she had hit pay dirt. He was a big-time movie producer, so he would have known Felicity through that channel. Once again, Regina was stereotyping, but she thought that movie producers tended to be misogynistic, for the casting couch was still a thing, and a lot of producers had been caught up in the whole #metoo dragnet. She thought the movie industry was still a good old boy industry, where women were treated as so much cattle.

It also made sense to her that if Felicity knew the person who raped her was a movie producer, she would be less likely to bring him down. That would completely explain why Felicity was suddenly eager to testify against Jamel – she was probably being pressured to do so. It also made a lot more sense, because this guy was local and Max was not. Not that Max would not end up in California at some point, but it made a lot more sense that Felicity was raped by somebody she knew. It would be very difficult for a rando, even a high-powered rando such as Max, to get at Felicity, but somebody like Noel would have easy access to her. It all added up when Regina found out what Noel did.

And as she watched Dallas's reaction to her saying that Noel Harrison was the rapist, she had no doubt she was on to something.

He licked his lips some more, and his bony fingers started to shake. "Why would Noel Harrison do something like that?" he asked.

"Why, indeed? Why does anybody do things like that? Obviously, the guy is fucked up. In the head. It doesn't have to be rational, but I would say that there's something in his background that's causing him to be violent. Not that that excuses anything, of course, because it doesn't. But why do I think that holy-rolling pious hypocrite, Timothy Harrison, is primarily responsible for fucking up his son? Anyhow, that's neither here nor there, but we need to bring this guy down. I mean, he did that to Felicity. Do you think she was the first one? Do you think she's going to be the last? How long before this guy actually starts murdering women? It's a logical next step - leave no witnesses and all of that. Could you live with something like that on your head? Because if you can't, then you have no business pleading Jamel guilty tomorrow. You plead him guilty, and that case is closed. If that case is closed, then that means the bastard got away with it. And if he gets away with it, he's going to keep doing it. That's a fact. Guys like that just don't stop. So do you want to be responsible for women dying because of this guy, or do you want to do the right thing and help me and Christian bring him down? It's a simple choice, really. Do the right thing or don't. Be responsible for women being raped, and maybe murdered, or be responsible for a guy going to prison who sorely needs to be there. Your choice."

Regina leaned back in her chair and watched Dallas closely. He was fidgeting, his fingers were shaking, and he looked like he wanted a drink very badly. He swallowed hard. "You say this Christian person can pay me $5000 upfront, and I'll just work it off, like a retainer?"

"That's what I'm saying. You in?"

"I'll be honest with you, I'm terrified. We're going up against the second-most powerful man in the country and one of the most powerful studio heads. I hope you know what you are doing."

"Oh, I know what I'm doing. Now, what I would like for you to do is withdraw from Jamel's case. Don't worry, we'll still be working on this case since you're going to be joining Christian. But you need to withdraw as his lead attorney. And then, once you withdraw, the judge will have no choice but to continue the plea agreement court appearance. And that will give me time to put my plan into action."

Dallas finally made a decision. "Okay. You're right. I have to do the right thing. I do need that money, though. I need for it to be put into my PayPal account, just like you said. I...have an emergency. My mother, she needs emergency surgery. Cancer. The doctors need a down payment, so I need that money today."

Regina almost called him out on that bull-shit lie, but thought better of it. "Whatever. You put in your withdraw motion, and you actually do withdraw, and you'll get your money. But not before then."

Regina left. She had work to do, and she would have to do it fast.

Chapter Twenty-One

REGINA

THE FIRST THING Regina did was talk to some pimps that she knew on the street. She had a feeling this guy had made the rounds, probably buying hookers and working them over. She needed to show the picture of Noel around to all the working girls she could possibly talk to, to see how many of them knew him, and how many of them would be willing to speak out against him. She had a feeling that any one woman was not going to be willing to do anything, but there was always safety in numbers, and that meant she had to gather them together as a group. So she had to get in touch with some pimps and see what she could do about showing Noel's picture around to the working girls under them.

BY THE END of two weeks of constantly interviewing one working girl after another, Regina had a group of 20 women willing to speak out against Noel, on the condition that all of them spoke with one voice.

Then, it was a matter of getting together the press, because she would call a press conference and put this guy on blast, once and for all.

Regina had some contacts with the Los Angeles press, but that was not enough. She needed national attention. This was too big to keep local. So she called a local reporter by the name of Harry Higgins, who was hooked in with some national reporters and some of the big-name television shows on cable TV, and asked him if he could pull some strings to get her press conference covered nationally.

"You're going to be accusing, on TV, the son of the vice president, who also happens to be a powerful studio head himself, of being a serial rapist of hookers. Trust me, if you can provide these women, I'll provide the national exposure," Harry said.

"They're going to speak."

Regina was nervous, because all these women were working girls, hookers, and she knew they were all going to be ripped apart by the media. She knew these women did not have credibility, but it would be undeniable what they were saying. They were going to speak with one voice and Regina hoped that voice would be powerful.

Then, one night when she was working in her Los Angeles office, the office that Christian had opened up for her in Santa Monica, she got a phone call.

"Hello, I heard you were going to be holding a press conference about Noel Harrison?" a very timid voice said to Regina on the phone.

"Yes, you heard right. I'm going to hold a press conference three days from now, and these women are going to be my stars. There's 20 of them. How did you find out about it?"

Regina was trying to keep the whole press conference scenario under wraps, because she did not want to tip off Noel or anybody around him. She was afraid that if he found out about what she would do, he would get to every single one of those women and put all of them in danger. Regina had to have the press conference, and then she knew the women would be safe, because if any one of them turned up dead after they told their story to the media, the first person that everybody would be looking at would be Noel. The second person would be Timothy. But, if either man, or anybody associated with Noel, got wind of what was about to happen, that the press conference would go on, nobody would be safe.

So, it somewhat disturbed Regina that this woman, whoever she was, had heard about the press conference.

"I found out about it because I'm a friend of Harry's. He told me. And he told me not to tell anybody. But I had to call you when I found out."

"Okay. And you are?"

"My name is Jacqueline Foster. I was a UCLA student when Noel Harrison raped me."

Chapter Twenty-Two

REGINA

REGINA COULD BARELY CONTAIN her excitement. It was one thing to hold a press conference with 20 working girls. It was another to get a, for lack of a better word, more respectable woman to join the chorus. Regina hated to think of the working girls as being less-than a college student, a college graduate by now, but she knew the reality – even if Regina did not look down on the working girls, society did. Society looked down on them, and society was less likely to believe what they said.

But if she could get somebody who was a UCLA student when she was raped? That would be powerful.

"Can we meet? I need to talk to you."

"Yes. I would love to meet. I've been carrying around this burden for all these years, wondering about how much violence I unleashed onto the world because I did not press charges against him when he did what he did to me. I took a very large settlement to keep quiet. But my doing that has haunted me all these years. I've talked to some attorneys, and I know the contract I signed, where I volunteered to not press charges against that man in exchange for $200,000, is void because it's against public policy. The consideration I gave in exchange for the money, which was a promise not to press criminal charges, is not valid consideration. So, I think I'm okay on the contract front, but even if I'm not, and I'm forced to pay back that money, so be it. I just can't live with the guilt anymore."

"Okay, let's meet. Where would you like to meet?"

"How about a place called Pomodoro Trattoria? It's close to where I work, which is UCLA. I'm an associate professor of literature there."

Even better. Professors get believed and they get results.

"What time, I'll be there."

"How about 8 PM?"

"You got it."

Chapter Twenty-Three

REGINA

AT 8 O'CLOCK, Regina showed up at the restaurant, but she didn't know who she was looking for. Fortunately, Prof. Foster apparently did. She stood up and waved when Regina walked in the door. Regina made a beeline for the table where Prof. Foster was sitting.

"How did you know what I looked like?" Regina asked.

"Harry told me what you looked like. He said you're a knockout, but I have to say, that description does not do you justice."

"Thanks," Regina said. "You're not so bad yourself." And that was not a lie. Jacqueline was a tall, willowy blonde, with big blue eyes and a Barbie doll face. She was athletic, with broad shoulders and strong legs that were highlighted by the casual khaki shorts she was wearing. She closely resembled Felicity, and Regina knew Noel definitely had a physical type. For even as Felicity and Jacqueline looked very similar, they also looked strikingly like many of the working girls that Regina had managed to round up. The working girls were all ethnicities and ages, but the blonde ones looked like this woman.

"So tell me what I need to do. I'll do anything at this point."

"I need for you to speak at this press conference. That's what I need. Sunlight will be the only disinfectant in this case. So far, I've only managed to gather together prostitutes. Which is fine, because there's 20 of them, and they're all going to speak. The media is going to dismiss him, just because of what they do. But you're a professor. They're going to listen to you. Even if this guy is the son of the vice-president. They're going to hear what you have to say. And if you speak, there's a chance that Felicity will be part of the press conference as well. I've talked to her, and she won't do it. She's afraid of Noel, afraid of what he could do to her career, but, if you want to know the truth, I think that mainly she does not want to be speaking in front of the press with a bunch of working girls. But if you decide to get in front of the microphone, Felicity might as well. So are you game for that? It's in three days. I'm going to have people from every national media source there, *CNN, MSNBC, Fox News, The Wall Street Journal, The Washington Post, The New York Times,* and *The Guardian* in Great Britain. They're all going to be there. It's going to be a circus sideshow, but it's important that this happens. This guy has been intimidating people for long enough. He's been getting away with it for long enough. It's time that all of that stops."

"What if he sues?"

"For what? Defamation of character? Slander? He won't sue. If he sues, there's going to be a discovery process, and the discovery process will not work in his favor. Trust me on this. He'll threaten everybody with a lawsuit, but I know for a fact that he's not going to want to go through with it, because once the other attorney does discovery, and depositions are taken, he's not only going to not have a leg to stand on, but he's going to have all his dirty laundry aired. He's going to want to have this thing buried as soon as possible, but I'm not going to let him. I'm going to use this press conference to put pressure on the prosecutor's office to press charges against him for all of these rapes. He may or may not be convicted, hopefully he will be, but it's going to be great for all of the women he has wronged to have their day in court. So don't worry about him suing. You're going to be fine."

"But what if he kills us, or has us killed?"

"That's the beauty of the press conference. He won't be able to lay a glove on any of you girls, because if he does, or if he has somebody he hires lay a glove on any of you, he'll be first person they look at. And if the prosecutor's office refuses to look at him for anybody's harm in the future, there will be an outcry in the public such as you have never heard. That's the whole purpose of this press conference - this guy has gotten away with it because of who he is, but, once the public knows what he did, there's going to be enormous pressure to actually put this guy behind bars. That's why I say that sunlight on this case will be the best disinfectant. The only disinfectant. And you can be a part of this. I would like for you to be a part of this."

Jacqueline took a deep breath. "I have a lot to lose. I mean, I've seen what happens when women go against powerful men in public. They start getting death threats. They have to move from their house. Their life is never their own again."

"I understand that, but the alternative is that this guy continues to get away with it. And it's only a matter time before he starts killing. I know you don't want that on your head. I know you feel bad about the fact that if you would have spoken up when Noel did that to you, Felicity would've never been a victim. Not to mention all the other nameless, faceless women he made victims since he raped you. He's going to keep on doing it. As long as people enable him, he will keep doing it. I know you're afraid. I know you're scared. I know you realize that doing this will turn your life upside down. But, as the song says, I want to see you be brave."

Jacqueline nodded her head. "Yes. Yes I will be a part of your press conference."

Chapter Twenty-Four

CHRISTIAN

I GOT off the phone with Regina, who informed me that, in addition to 20 prostitutes who had suffered at the hands of Noel Harrison, she also had a professor by the name of Jacqueline Foster who was willing to speak out as well.

When I heard that, I jumped for joy. Jamel's case was still active, and Jamel himself was still in jail, awaiting trial. I managed to put my appearance in, after Dallas withdrew, and the first thing I did was take it off the plea docket. I had a talk with Jamel, and told him that, while it was tempting for him to take an offer, I advised strongly against it. I just could not, in good conscience, advise an innocent kid to take any plea deal, no matter how strong the evidence was against him.

When I found out a professor would speak out, the first thing I did was call Felicity. I knew, after she had spoken with me, that she was persuadable. Even though she was willing to lie and testify against Jamel, I still knew that, in her heart, she was on my side. It was just a matter of maybe giving her a push. I mean, she gave me her private cell phone number. To me, that meant she was willing to work with me, even if she was afraid.

She answered the phone. "Hello, Christian, what can I do for you?"

Christian took a deep breath. What if he told Felicity about the press conference, and she, instead of being open to doing it with the others, actually sabotaged it by telling everybody it was about to happen? If the principles in this case, including the vice president, and Noel himself, ever got wind that this would happen, they could probably stop it. They could probably squash it and then they would probably be able to silence everybody. It was imperative they not know about the press conference ahead of time. So I would have to take a gamble that Felicity wouldn't speak to the vice president and the others about what was about to happen.

Here goes nothing.

"I wanted to call you because I wanted to invite you to be a part of a press conference taking place on Thursday. Three days from now. It's a press conference that's going to be held by all the women that Noel Harrison beat and raped. It's going to be mainly prostitutes, but there will be one professor who's going to speak out as well. I wanted to give you the chance to do the right thing, once and for all, and tell the world your story. Tell the world your story, and, while you're at it, you'll be making sure my client, an innocent man, goes free, once and for all. Obviously, taking part in this press conference will be your choice. But I wanted to give you the opportunity to make that choice."

I could hear Felicity breathing on the other end. "Is this press conference going forward, with or without my participation?"

"Yes. It is."

"In other words, after Thursday, the media's going to go ape shit on the story. And everybody's going to know what kind of a monster Noel Harrison is? And the public will pressure prosecutors to bring charges against him? And there's probably going to be congressional hearings about this, because, after all, this guy is the son of the vice president? Is that what you're telling me?"

"Yes. That's exactly what I'm telling you. No matter what, the press conference will go. So you can either be a part of it, or not. I would like for you to be a part of it, and I would like for you to, after you take part in this, go to the prosecutor and ask them to dismiss the case against Jamel Jackson with prejudice. That means they cannot ever bring it up against him again. That's what I would like for you to do."

Felicity got quiet, so quiet I could hear her breathing. "I want to do that, believe me, I do. I just don't know what it's going to do to my career. You don't know how powerful that guy is in this town. He's going to blackball me. I won't be able to get another job in Hollywood, ever. He has the power to bury me, and he will. He will."

Hmm. She used to be afraid for her life. Obviously, if she took part in the press conference, she wouldn't have to fear for her life anymore. If anything happened to her, if she was murdered, vice president Harrison and Noel Harrison would be the first people implicated. The public would make sure these two men paid for doing anything to Felicity after she spoke out.

So, her life wouldn't be in danger if she took part in the press conference, but her career would be. How shallow could she be to let something like that deter her from doing the right thing?

I had to take some deep breaths to keep me from jumping through the phone and strangling her.

"Felicity," I began, "there are lives at stake here. We don't know when this guy will escalate into murder. Maybe he already has. At any rate, he's a serial rapist. He's been a serial rapist, apparently for years. We have the chance to make sure he's behind bars, but that chance relies on the public getting enough up in arms that the prosecutor's office in LA has to charge that bastard. The only way for the public to get riled up is if they know about what happened. You can not only add your voice to this chorus, but you can be the most powerful speaker there. You have the most to lose in speaking out, which means you will have the most credibility out of anyone there. If you're not there, the press conference will go on, but it certainly will be much less effective. If you're there, it's a guarantee this matter will get the attention it deserves, both from the media and from the public. Please, think about it."

"I will. I will. Listen, I have to get off the phone. I'm in the middle of shooting a scene and they're calling me to go onto the set to shoot it. The press conference is at what time on Thursday?"

"3 PM. It will be on the steps of the Los Angeles Courthouse. I hope to see you there."

"I hope so too. I really do. I just don't know if I have the courage to go through with it."

"At least you're no longer testifying against Jamel. At least you are no longer going to lie to the court about him. I guess that's the least I can ask of you."

She got very quiet and I could hear her crying. "I can't believe I was going to do that. I was desperate, you see. Noel was calling me, 24/7, pressuring me to testify against Jamel, threatening me with violence and threatening me with blackballing me from the industry. I panicked. I'm so glad that guilty plea never happened, though. If that guilty plea would have gone through because that poor kid was afraid I was going to testify against him, I would have never been able to live with myself."

"You'll be able to live with yourself much more if you do the right thing here," I said, stating the obvious. "You'll be able to sleep at night again. You'll be able to look your children in the eye, when you have them, and you'll be able to tell them that, when it mattered, you took the hard way, the painful way, but the right way. You'll be able to be a role model for them. Think of it that way."

More silence. "Thanks, I'll think about it. Bye."

At that, she hung up.

Chapter Twenty-Five

CHRISTIAN

THURSDAY CAME, and Regina and I were standing on the Los Angeles Courthouse steps, flanked by the prostitutes who were going to speak their piece, along with Jacqueline, who looked awkwardly around her. She looked like she was afraid somebody would jump out of the bushes at her and assault her.

Maybe she *was* afraid of that, I don't know.

As for the prostitutes, they all managed to clean up very nicely for this event. Several of them had called Regina, anxious about what they were supposed to wear, how much makeup should they put on, what about their hair, and Cecilia just got a new weave that looked like a bird's nest, should she have it taken out before the presser? Regina, for her part, helped each of them choose a demure dress and the ones who were having issues because their hair was too big, or too thin, or too curly, were taken to various hairdressers, who gave all of the ones with hair issues haircuts that were flattering yet conservative.

At the moment, they were lined up behind Regina,

many of them blonde – Noel certainly had a type, and it was tall, thin blondes – all of them dressed in conservative-ish dresses and pantsuits, all of them looking like they wanted to be anywhere but there. Several of them were staring out with wide eyes at the sea of satellite trucks, the reporters on the street with microphones, and the crowd that was gathering, no-doubt wondering what all the fuss was about. A couple of them had tears in those eyes.

No doubt about it, the scene was building along with the crowd. I started to feel a tinge of apprehension myself, although I was sure my sense of foreboding was nothing compared to the ladies'.

It was 2:30 and the presser would begin at 3. I scanned the crowd, looking for Felicity, and I didn't see her anywhere. *Looks like she's going to take the cowardly way out after all.* Still, she didn't rat us out and tell Noel and Vice-President Harrison what was about to happen, so I supposed I needed to be grateful for small favors.

I turned my back and Samantha, one of the accusers, pointed. "Look at that," she said. "That actress lady is here. Felicity something, she's here."

I turned back around and saw Felicity McDaniel weaving through the crowd. It was difficult for her to do, of course, as everybody with a microphone was wanting to talk to her, and the people in the crowd who were fans of hers were trying to get her autograph. It was therefore slow-going.

But she was there. She showed up.

She finally made her way to the podium. "I'm not late, am I?" she asked.

"No, you're not late. In fact, it's 5 till 3 now. So you're early."

"Early," she said. "Nobody has ever accused me of

being early to places. I guess there's a first time for everything, huh?"

"Yes," I said. "I guess so."

She nodded. "I couldn't sleep last night again. And I realized you were right. I think my chronic insomnia has something to do with the fact that I've been such a candyass about this whole thing. My mother didn't raise me to do things like let monsters get away with being monsters, not when I have a chance to actually do something about it. I mean, who cares if I'm blackballed from Hollywood? I came from nothing. I was working at a Starbucks before I got my first modeling gig, when I wasn't waiting tables at various restaurants. I have skills to fall back on. I make a mean caramel latte, let me tell you. And there's always Broadway. I get booted out of this town and I'll seek the lights of Broadway. If Broadway is good enough for Chris Evans and Denzel Washington, it's good enough for me."

"Thank you for coming," I said. "You don't know how much of an impact this will have, especially now that you're going to speak your truth."

She nodded her head. "I feel sick," she said. "But I went over what I would say, just like I go over my lines before a scene. So I'm not going to mess up."

3 PM came and I went over to the microphone. "Hello, everybody," I said. "I suppose everybody here is curious about what this presser is all about."

I tried to ignore the popping flashbulbs and all the reporters who were standing right in front me, in rapt attention. Like Felicity, I started to feel nauseated. I had never in my life done anything this enormous, this nationwide, and I really felt like I would faint.

Still, I pressed on. "These women that are up here with me, they all have one thing in common. They were all victims of a vicious rape by Noel Harrison. You know Noel Harrison as the oldest son of the vice-president of the United States, Timothy Harrison. You also know Mr. Harrison as one of the most powerful studio heads in Hollywood. These ladies behind me simply know him as the man who viciously assaulted them. Several of these ladies were left for dead, including Felicity McDaniel, the legendary actress here today to tell her truth, along with the other ladies who are not as famous as Ms. McDaniel, but who are just as courageous. Every single woman will tell her truth, her story, and you won't be able to look away. But you don't need to hear me talk the entire time. You need to hear these ladies' stories. So, I present to you, Samantha Dowell."

Samantha came to the podium, and she took the hand of the lady standing next to her and gripped it tightly. She took a deep breath and proceeded to tell her story.

One by one, the ladies took the podium, got up to the microphone, and told the crowd and throngs of reporters what had happened to them at the hands of the vicious and sadistic monster known at Noel Harrison. They told stories of being beaten, kicked, and raped. Several of them ended up in the hospital due to their injuries. Several of them told the reporters and crowd about how they were affected by what had happened to them.

"Don't get me wrong, I'm used to rough treatment," said Clarissa, a 33-year-old prostitute currently working a street in North Hollywood. "But this was something else. This was the vicious work of somebody who is violent and hates women. Hates them. He wanted to kill me. I know he did. I only survived because I got to the hospital on time. If I didn't, I wouldn't be here today."

Every woman told the same type of story. They worked the streets, and they always knew they were taking their lives into their hands. But they never had encountered somebody quite like Noel Harrison.

Jacqueline then told her story. I decided to put her next to last, with Felicity being the last person to speak. The crowd got quiet as she approached the microphone. "My name is Jacqueline Foster," she said. "And I was an 18-year-old freshman at UCLA when Noel Harrison raped me. I was walking home from a party one night. Maybe I had a few. I was by myself when a man leaped out from behind some bushes and put his hand over my mouth. He dragged me off the sidewalk and into a wooded area. There, he pulled down my jeans and raped me. He beat me after he raped me, and left me for dead. I played like I was dead so he would leave me alone, and he did, thank God. After he left, I managed to drag myself out of the woods and hail a passing car. They took me to the hospital. I had a concussion, contusions on my face, my left eye was swollen shut. I had internal injuries from being kicked in my abdomen, again and again.

Since that time, I have been unable to have a normal life. I have not had a normal relationship with a man since that time. I have nightmares every single night. I've tried to commit suicide twice. I've suffered from drug addiction and alcoholism, both of which I've kicked with the help of my mother and father and with help from the Almighty. I've managed to finish my PhD, so I'm an associate professor at UCLA, but finishing this degree has taken every ounce of spare energy from me. I don't think I will ever marry, have children, or be able to sleep through the night without waking up screaming. My physical wounds have healed, but my mental ones will never do the same. This man is a monster and he needs to be stopped."

At that, she faded back with the others and gripped

hands with two of the other ladies. Every lady was, by this time, holding hands with each other, both as a show of solidarity and as a comfort.

Finally, it was Felicity's turn to speak. She looked uncomfortably out into the crowd, but she took the microphone into her hand and brought it to her mouth. "Hello," she said. "I'm Felicity McDaniel. Most of you might know me from my movie roles and my Netflix series. My story is much the same as these other ladies. Noel Harrison stalked me for some time. He would always show up at my home, at all hours of the night, and I couldn't get rid of him. I always thought that he was harmless, however, and my agent told me I needed to not ask him to leave. I needed to be accommodating of him when he showed up, because if I wasn't accommodating, I would lose my status in Hollywood. Noel Harrison had the power to break me if he wanted to. He still does. So, as I speak to you right now, know that I'm doing this at the risk of losing my career. I have everything to lose by doing this, so you all know I'm speaking the truth.

You've read about what happened to me. Everybody knows about how I was raped, beaten and left for dead next to my pool. How I was in the hospital for weeks, without a memory of what had happened. But that's not entirely true. I had a memory of what happened, but I was too afraid to speak about it. Too afraid that if I stuck up my head, I would get it chopped off. Too afraid of what would happen to me if everybody knew the truth. So I was silent when an innocent 18-year-old boy was taken into custody for raping me. I was silent when that same boy was convicted for my rape. I pretended I didn't know who raped me, so that boy, Jamel Jackson, was just as likely as anybody else to have done it, so who was I to speak up and tell the world differently about him?"

Felicity took a breath and wiped away some tears. "That was a lie. I knew Noel Harrison was the man who raped me. I remembered him doing it. I will never forget that day, never in a million years. The way he viciously pummeled my face while screaming, over and over again, about how angry he was that I wouldn't take him as my lover. He called me a whore, a slut, a dirty woman. He bit me on my breast, taking out a chunk of flesh. He anal-raped me, and I had never been penetrated there, so the pain was excruciating. After he was finished, he left me there. If it weren't for Jamel Jackson showing up when he did by that pool, I would be dead. Of that, I'm certain. As it was, I was near-death when I got to the hospital. I had lost a great amount of blood and I had massive internal injuries. I was in surgery for 7 hours while the doctors heroically did all they could to make sure I didn't bleed out, either internally or externally. All the while, I knew who did this. I knew who did this, yet I stood by and let an innocent boy take the fall.

I could never live with myself if I didn't do something to make sure that boy did not get convicted again of my assault and if I never told my story when I had the chance. I never felt I had the chance to tell anybody about what had happened to me, because I was afraid of what Noel would do to me if I told. I was terrified that I would never work again if I said anything. I feared for my life. It was only when I was told these other women would be here too, all of them speaking their truth in solidarity, that I decided that I, too, must speak my truth. I, too, must tell my story. And I am firmly ready to swallow the consequences that will be associated with my being here today to tell the world about what Noel Harrison did to me. Thank you very much."

After she was through speaking, you could hear a pin drop on the sidewalk. Then, all at once, everybody was talking, trying to get closer to Felicity so they could get some exclusive words from her. The reporters weren't satisfied to have been in the crowd, listening to the great Felicity McDaniel expound about her vicious assault at the hands of the son of the current VP. They all wanted to get some exclusive words from her, too, something that nobody else would be reporting on. They all wanted the scoop.

So Felicity was mobbed, while the other women remained behind the dais, holding hands with one another. One of the women started to sing the lyrics from *Brave* by Sara Bareilles, while the other women picked up the chorus and sang along. After that song ended, another woman started singing the Lady Gaga song, *'Til It Happens to You*, her song about her own rape, and some of the ladies who knew that song sang along.

The ladies stood there, with flashbulbs popping and reporters clamoring, singing song after song about female empowerment and surviving. None of them talked to the multitude of reporters who were done with Felicity and were now eager to talk to all the other women.

They said their piece, and they were done.

Chapter Twenty-Six

CHRISTIAN

THE NEXT DAY, I woke up to see the presser was leading every single news station, both locally and nationally, and I knew I had done my job. This was the vice-president's son at the crucible of this particular story, and nobody would let that go, especially since he was so wealthy and powerful in his own right.

That was behind me and I had a more important job to do.

I went directly to the prosecutor's office and marched into Matthew Howard's office. I didn't have an appointment, but I felt I didn't need one.

He looked up at me when I came into his office. "Christian," he said. "I just filed, on-line, my notice of dismissal for Jamel's case. With prejudice. Of course."

I nodded. "You're damned right it's with prejudice. How can you live with yourself, doing that to an innocent kid? I mean, really, how do you look in the mirror?"

He sighed. "It was the vice-president's son. I couldn't-"

"Yes you could. You could have done the right thing and

prosecuted him, but you didn't. Now the whole world knows about what you did. The whole world knows you railroaded an innocent boy to cover up for Noel Harrison's crimes and you were prepared to railroad him again, even after his conviction was overturned. Was that really a better outcome for you? If you would have done the right thing, you would have been a hero. As it is, everyone knows you're nothing but a lily-livered, candyassed coward. Have a nice life."

He didn't say a word to me as I turned and left. How could he? He had no defense. Zero. There was nothing he could possibly say that wouldn't make his situation worse, so he obviously chose to say nothing at all.

And that was fine.

Those ladies said all that needed to be said.

Now it was up to Matthew Howard to do the right thing and put that bastard into prison, where he belonged.

I only hoped he found enough courage to do it.

Epilogue

THREE WEEKS after the presser and I finally saw what I had been hoping to see - a perp walk. Noel Harrison was being frog-marched out of his office in handcuffs while the press, having been tipped off about what would happen, went nuts on the street in front of his luxury building.

It was a long time coming. Too long. I was surprised it had actually happened, considering all the strings VP Harrison was trying to pull on behalf of his son. He was threatening to cut aid to California, with the excuse that California mismanages federal dollars, but the real story was that he was only threatening that because he wanted the state of California to back off of charging his son. Everybody knew it. Everybody called him on it. Some people in his party made excuses for him, of course, but none of the excuses rang true anymore.

Weeks of public protests were what finally forced the prosecutor's hands. Every single day, thousands of people showed up on the steps of the prosecutor's office, with signs and bullhorns, and made their voices heard. Politicians came to their aid, as many senators, congressmen and women would show up at these protests and speak to the crowd. Politicians from both sides of the aisle actually participated in the blood-letting, which just showed the VP wasn't as powerful as he might've thought.

Finally, the prosecutor's office knew they couldn't ignore it any longer. They were defeated. They would have to finally take that guy into custody. So, they coordinated with the local police to do their business, and do it, they did.

Whether or not he would be convicted for his crimes was unknown. I had to hope he would be. Felicity would be a powerful voice in court, just as powerful as she was in that press conference. So would Jacqueline. So would all the nameless, faceless prostitutes he viciously assaulted.

As for VP Harrison? He was being replaced when the president was going to run for re-election. He was finished. His political career was dead. It wasn't just that he raised a monster - it was that he created that monster. After the press conference, journalists started to dig, and what they found was that Noel had suffered horrific abuse at the hands of his pious, religious father. Details of that abuse filled the tabloids, magazines, blogs, social media and nightly news programs.

Then details started to come out about all the money VP Harrison had paid over the years to women his son assaulted. It turned out he not only paid off Jacqueline, but also a few prostitutes who were going to go to the police about what Noel did - they weren't scared, like some of the others were, and they were going to tell their story. Suddenly, they were off the streets, with large bank accounts, and their mouths were shut. All of this came out, cascading through legacy and social media, as everybody pounced on this salacious story like sharks tearing through chum.

Jamel was beyond grateful, of course. He was back with Uber but eyeing a career in auto mechanics. Felicity agreed to help him with the financial part of his schooling - she set up a large scholarship just for him. He was calling me every week, giving me a status report, telling me that he was excited about something for the first time in his life.

As for me...well, I had the satisfaction that I saved a boy from injustice. It was only one boy. There were millions of others like him. But I saved him, and that gave me a great sense of satisfaction.

Almost as much satisfaction as I felt when I watched that bastard being perp-walked.

Almost.

Next in the Southern California Legal Thrillers Series

vinci-books.com/the-trial

A dying boy. A corrupt corporation. Avery's quest for justice in the face of insurmountable odds.

When seven-year-old Frankie Jamison is diagnosed with a lethal disease, his mother Lorinda turns to her friend Regina for help. Desperate for answers, Regina enlists Avery to investigate the cause of Frankie's illness. As Avery delves deeper into the case, she uncovers a web of corporate greed and corruption that stretches far beyond anything she could have imagined.

Turn the page for a free preview…

The Trial: Chapter One

LORINDA

October 15

LORINDA JAMISON DID the Chinese splits on stage right in front of a well-dressed guy with dark hair, blue eyes, and a big smile. He had been drinking at the strip bar where she worked, since 9 o'clock in the morning, and it was now probably around 2 or so. Lorinda had no idea what time it was, as this bar, like most bars like it, had no clocks. It was also always dark inside, so, no matter what time of the day it was, it always felt like midnight to Lorinda.

Then again, her life always felt like midnight.

She lay down on her stomach, with her legs splayed out behind her, and the good-looking guy, who now was completely schnockered, playfully put a $20 bill into her bustier. He looked right at her and licked his lips.

Lorinda took a deep breath, feeling the sense of burnout that she had been feeling for quite a while. It wasn't necessarily that she hated what she was doing. On the contrary, being an exotic dancer was actually a job that gave her a sense of satisfaction. She had to keep her body in shape, otherwise there was no way in hell she could do the acrobatics on the pole she was able to perform – her legs, which were strong enough to crack a walnut, would be clutching the stripper pole, while the rest of her body hung down, a movement much harder than it looked. Well, maybe – because she knew it looked damned difficult. All those middle-aged housewives who took pole dancing a few years back had no idea what they were in for. That was probably why that particular exercise fad faded away so quickly, because hardly anybody could do what she and the other dancers could do.

It wasn't just the fact that she took a special pride in her body and what it could do on stage, but also the fact that she felt powerful over the men who would come to see her, that gave her such satisfaction. It was a special sense of giving them what they wanted, but only up to a point, teasing them, making them think she was into them, so they would give her $20 tips instead of $10 ones. In reality, not one of those guys would ever have a chance with her, no matter what he looked like, and no matter what he did. She was a one-man woman, and that man's name was Frankie. Well, she wasn't really a one-man woman, so much as she was a one-boy woman – Frankie, at the age of seven, certainly could not qualify as being a man.

But, then again, Frankie was more mature than any of the guys she met at this club.

Frankie was why she was feeling a sense of burnout. She wanted to be with him a lot more than she was. Most of the time, because she had been working at this club for so long, she could choose her hours, and she would choose the hours Frankie was in school. He went to elementary school at 8:30 in the morning and would be home around 3:30 every afternoon. So she chose to work those particular hours. She knew she would still get quite a lot of business even during the day, because that was how it usually was. There were quite a few men who would come in during the lunch hour, for a little escapist fantasy in the middle of the day, along with probably quite a few men who'd told their wives they were at the office but were really spending the day stuffing her bra and G-String with $20 bills. So, even though she did not work at night, she still made some good money while Frankie was in school.

That all worked out very well until recently.

Now, Frankie was not in school. He was at home and she wanted to be with him.

The handsome guy with the dark hair was still staring at her, his perfect teeth gleaming in the glow of the bar. He winked at her and took another drink. "How would you like to go with me into a private room?" he asked her, slurring his words. "I could very much make it worth your while."

She didn't necessarily want to do that, because she knew what men expected when they went to the private room. Not that they were entitled to it. But they seemed to have the attitude that if they were going to pay her the rate the club charged for these private rooms, they expected to get something in return. But she'd been working at the club for long enough to know that she did not have to do what she didn't want to.

And this club had a very strict "no touch" policy - the men were never to touch the dancers, except to put money in their g-strings and bras. Still, the men always expected to be able to not just touch the dancers, but get sexual favors as well. That was why Lorinda hated going back into the private rooms.

When she first started working there, she had to go into

these private rooms when they asked her. She had no choice in the matter. But now, she could say no, and her boss would not be upset with her.

She thought about Frankie, about what he needed. That was literally the only thing she ever thought about anymore. She knew that with his illness, she needed to make as much money as possible. The hospital bills were starting to really mount up and she was having an argument with the insurance company as it was. She could not afford a decent insurance policy for Frankie and she made slightly more than the threshold to be eligible for the Child Health Insurance Program, commonly known as CHIP, which was available to people who made $31,000 or under a year. So she had to go to the free market to get her insurance payment plan for him, while she did not have insurance at all. The most she could afford was a plan with a $15,000 deductible and co-pays for everything. She never imagined she would be blowing through that deductible so quickly, but then again, she never imagined she would have a child who would come down with a very rare form of cancer. Mesothelioma, which was caused by exposure to asbestos, was rare in adults, and exceedingly rare in children of Frankie's age.

In fact, his cancer was so rare that the doctors wanted to treat him with experimental drugs, because, as of now, there wasn't much of a treatment protocol for what he had. At least, there was not yet a treatment protocol for young children with the disease. Even Frankie's subtype of mesothelioma was rarer than rare - he had the disease in the lining of his heart, and this particular type of cancer had affected so few children that there was very little research done on it, so her doctors were shooting in the dark.

It didn't help that she could not afford to see a specialist, because the one specialist who knew something about Frankie's kind of cancer was located at the Mayo Clinic in Minnesota. Traveling to Minnesota was a nonstarter for Lorinda, especially because her insurance company wouldn't pay for it. She could barely get them to pay for treatments he was going through right here in San Diego. If they would've paid for the specialist, she would've definitely tried to make some sacrifices to make it work. She would've done anything to help her son. But her insurance company had made it clear they were not going to pay for the specialist, so she had to make do with the doctors right there in San Diego, the doctors who had never seen a case of a child Frankie's age with the type of cancer he had, so they had no idea what they were doing when they were treating him.

So, she worked. She did whatever she had to do to get the money together to pay for her living expenses, and Frankie's. She took in a roommate, Sherry, who worked the night shift, from 8 PM to 3:30 in the morning, and she had a kid too, so the agreement was that Lorinda would watch Sherry's kid when Sherry went to work, in exchange for Sherry watching Frankie during the hours that Lorinda was in the bar working. Because Frankie was home most days, instead of being in school, because he just did not have the energy to get out of bed, Lorinda needed somebody to care for him while she was at work. And it worked out, because the two roommates were able to split the rent on a three-bedroom apartment, which was everything to her, as San Diego was not known to be a reasonably- priced city as far as rent goes. So Lorinda thought it was two birds one stone, in that she had a sitter for her kid and somebody to split expenses with her.

She reluctantly went to the private room with the dark-haired guy, who told her his name was Robert, but she had a feeling that was just a name he was giving her. A name he pulled out of a hat.

She noticed his left hand was sporting a very conspicuous tan line around his ring finger. She had to have a chuckle about that, because who did he think he was fooling? And who cares? The answer to that was nobody, but she could not afford to call him on his bullshit. Literally. She decided to do what she had to do - get through it and hopefully earn the hundred dollar or more tip she would get from being back there with him.

About an hour later, she emerged from the private room, $500 richer, and trying to forget what she let him do in that room. She closed her eyes and saw her only motivation for doing any of this.

Her boss, Michelangelo, found her and told her it was time for her to go home. "Your shift has been over for the past half hour, so it's time for you to clock out."

She breathed a sigh of relief and then went back into the dressing room, and put on her regular clothes – jeans, T-shirt, and a battered pair of Converse running shoes, a relic from the days when she was a marathon runner. Sometimes she thought about those days, when she was a university student at the University of California San Diego, with the hopes of studying marine biology. That was before she found out she was pregnant with Frankie and had to drop out. She danced while at the University, so she dropped her classes in favor of the easy money she made at the club. She even danced when she was nine months pregnant, because she found there were quite a few men who had a fetish about seeing a pregnant woman with minimal clothing. Then, even after he was born, she was back to work within weeks, because she literally could not afford to do anything else.

When she started dancing, she never imagined it would be a long-term thing, but here she was, 8 years later, and she was still dancing.

She stepped out into the bright sunlight, which was always a shocking thing after having been in the bar for so many hours, and it always took her a few minutes to adjust to the light. Then she made her way to the bus stop, which was right across the street from her club, and waited for the first of two buses that would take her to her apartment in the neighborhood of Ocean Beach. She knew she was paying more for what she had, because she was close to the beach – the apartment she shared with Sherry was less than 1000 square feet, even though it was a three bedroom, which meant that every bedroom was tiny, as was the living room and the tiny galley kitchen. No dining room, so everybody ate on TV trays.

She knew she could get a much nicer place for what they were paying for their tiny apartment, which was $3500 a month, if she would be willing to live more inland. Maybe El Cajon or Lakeside or another suburb in East County. But she chose to live by the beach because Frankie loved the water. He always did, even when he was a tiny toddler. She would take him to the ocean and could not get him out of the water. His chubby legs would stomp with delight in the surf, and his tiny hands would clap together while he giggled and sat down in the sand. She had never seen so much joy in any one person as she saw in her son when he was in the water. Such joy was infectious to her, and made her laugh and smile, and uplifted her own spirits. So she decided she was never going to live very far away from the ocean, even if she had to pay a premium for the luxury.

This was more important than ever to her. She herself could take the beach or leave it. She didn't like the heat, the crowds, the sand getting into every crevice of her body. She always had to slather on a ton of sunscreen, for she was exceedingly fair, unlike Frankie, who apparently got his father's genes, as his father was a dark-eyed, dark-skinned Italian man who date-raped her on the only night she had agreed to go out with him. He never knew he had a son and he never would know that. There was no way that she would ever, ever, let Frankie know how he was conceived.

She knew it would be easier if she would have simply let Salvatore know that he had a son, and she could have demanded child support from him, probably a lot of child support from him, considering he was an heir to a fortune and was living off a massive trust fund. But she knew that any child support from him would mean he would have partial custody of him as well – he would deny he raped her, of course, and it would be "he said she said," so he probably would get at least 50% custody if he had to pay child support. She wasn't going to do that. Plus, she couldn't risk Frankie being around Salvatore's extended family - any family who would raise a rapist was not a family she wanted her child to be exposed to. For that matter, she would never want her child to be exposed to a rapist, period. And that's what Salvatore was – a rapist.

So she had to get along as a completely single mother, with no means of support except for herself. She had no real education to speak of, as she had to drop out of college when she was only a freshman. For now, dancing was her life, and she had to scrimp and save every penny, because she knew there was going to come a time she would age out of her chosen profession. She had no plan B, so she was going to have to have some kind of retirement fund to live off of. Now, with Frankie sick, and the doctor bills piling up, there really wasn't much that went into her retirement account, such as it was. No matter how many Roberts were willing to pay her $500 for an hour of private teasing in an isolated room, she could not get ahead.

She got home and immediately saw Sherry was laying on the couch, with her son, Eric, who was the same age as Frankie. Frankie was nowhere to be seen and Lorinda knew what that meant.

She went into the bedroom Frankie shared with Eric. The two boys had bunk beds, Frankie on bottom, Eric on top, Frankie with *Star Wars* bed sheets, Eric with *Avengers*, which was the opposite of their backpacks, as Eric had a *Star Wars* backpack, while Frankie had an *Avengers* backpack.

She sat down on the bed and put her hand on Frankie's forehead. He was fast asleep, and she knew that if she asked Sherry, she probably would tell her that he'd been sleeping all day. That was all he seemed to do anymore.

Oh, he had some good days, where he actually had the energy to go out to the beach, and stand in the water, although his legs never stomped in the water the way they did when he was a tiny baby, for that sense of joy and wonder had long since left him. Yet, on those rare early evenings when Frankie made it out to the beach, he managed a smile. Lorinda had no idea if the smiles that he plastered on his face when she took him out to the water were genuine smiles, or if he simply made happy facial expressions because he wanted to make her happy. She might never know the answer to that question, but she did know that Frankie was the kind of boy who would do anything to please her. And he knew, he had to have known, that his deteriorating medical condition was bringing her to the depths of despair. She tried to hide it, much like he tried to hide his pain and sadness from her. She was pretty good at faking smiles for him, which was why she strongly suspected his smiles were fake as well.

Sometimes she wanted to talk to him about his illness. She wanted him to not be afraid of what was probably going to happen to him. She wanted him to not fear death. Yet, she could never bring herself to have *that* talk with him. Every time she went into his room, with the determination that she was going to have that heart-to-heart, the lump in her throat caught so that she couldn't get any words out, and the two of them never did talk about the impending end of his young life.

He knew he was dying. Children always knew. He knew that most of the kids he'd met in the oncology ward during his hospital stays were, by and large, no longer around. Sometimes she thought that maybe he wanted to talk to her about what he was feeling, but he was a sensitive boy, and he knew that if he was frank with her and told her he knew he would die soon, she would break down. And he wasn't wrong. She *would* break down. She knew that, so the upshot was that neither she nor he ever had the talk about what was going to happen.

Looking at him as he lay in his bed, so tiny and breathing so hard, as the cancer had put him into heart failure, she was afraid he was going to measure his life in hours, not days or weeks as she had hoped. With every breath he took, it seemed like she held her own. His chest would rise, and rise, and rise again, before it fell. She had seen this pattern with her mother, right before her mother's own heart exploded in her chest.

She took a hold of his wrist and felt his pulse, which was thready and light, which seemed to contradict the enormous breaths he was taking in his sleep. She wondered if she should take him back to the ER, but she knew that if she took him to the ER every time she was concerned about his breathing pattern in his sleep that he would spend his entire life in the ER.

She finally tore herself away from Frankie's bed, and went into the living room, and sat next to Sherry and Eric. She took a deep breath, and willed back the tears.

"He's been asleep for most of the day," Sherry said to Lorinda. "I've been checking on him every half hour."

Lorinda looked at her hands, which were clasped so tightly together that her knuckles were white. "We're going to go through another round of chemo, which starts next week. I just hope that –"

She didn't want to say the next words. She didn't want to say out loud what she was thinking. For what she was thinking was that she hoped Frankie could live long enough to take his next round of chemo. That was what she always hoped for - just live long enough to get to his next treatment. None of it did much good, because his cancer was just so rare that nobody really knew how to treat it.

Sherry nodded. She knew the words that were unsaid. She knew.

"So, what are you guys watching?" Lorinda asked Sherry.

Sherry just shrugged. "I don't know, something on Netflix. Eric wanted to watch it."

At that, Eric gave Lorinda a dirty look, which told Lorinda that he was trying to watch the movie, whatever it was, and did not appreciate her talking. She decided to not say anything more, but to take a little walk to her favorite coffee shop, which was just down the street. She would be back before eight, which was when Sherry went to her own shift at the bar. Then she would watch both Eric and

Frankie while Sherry danced at the club until the wee hours of the morning.

The coffee shop she loved was called the OB Garden Cafe. It was a cute little place that was vegan/vegetarian, with high wood ceilings, hardwood floors, and an open-air patio that was dog friendly. She always tried to make the rooftop yoga on Sundays at four, whenever she wasn't working on Sundays, and she really liked to frequent this place because there often were dogs out on the patio that she could pet, and, since she could not have a dog of her own in her small apartment, she got her dog fix there by petting other people's pooches.

Before she sat down, she noticed a familiar face across the room. Regina Baldwin was a friend of her's from way back when. Regina used to work at the same club she worked at, also as an exotic dancer. But the last she heard, Regina left the dancing scene to strike out on her own as a private detective.

After Regina left the club, Lorinda didn't really talk to her that much, as what happens when people leave their place of employment. That always made her sad – you really get to know somebody, you really start feeling comfortable with sharing your innermost thoughts and secrets, then that person leaves, and, at first, you try to keep in touch, calling each other every few weeks, and having lunch once in a while. Then the calls get less frequent, you start making excuses not to have lunch, and so does the other person – you're both so busy that it's very hard to make time in your schedule – and then one day, you realize you haven't talked to the other person in quite a while.

At first, Lorinda tried to pretend she didn't see Regina. She just thought it would be an uncomfortable conversation, because, truth be told, she felt that she was more responsible for the friendship dropping than Regina was. She felt inferior that Regina was making something of herself while she, herself, stayed on at the bar, still dancing for money. She felt left behind. Every time Regina would tell her about all the exciting cases she was working, Lorinda felt a little stab of jealousy go through her heart. She knew in her gut, in her soul, that what she was doing at the moment was all that she would ever be doing. She didn't have the same kind of intelligence and talent Regina and some of the other girls who managed to make it out of the exotic dancing scene had. She didn't have the instincts or investigation skills that Regina had acquired, and she didn't have the kind of guts it took to be a private investigator. And she knew that Regina had another ace in the hole, that helped her get out of dancing for good – her friend, Avery Collins, a lawyer who was Regina's cellmate in prison. Avery took a chance on Regina and helped her break into the PI business.

Lorinda didn't have anybody to help her break into anything, so she really saw no way out of her dancing career. Regina made it out, so Lorinda didn't want to associate with her anymore. Regina just made her feel bad.

Unfortunately, or fortunately, depending on how you looked at it, Regina did notice Lorinda at the coffee shop. As Lorinda sat down, Regina came over to her table, and sat down as well.

"Hey, you, where you been hiding? You know, I've been trying to call you for quite a while, and you never answer your phone. Maybe I should take the hint, but I'm not one to take hints like that. So, how the hell are you?" Regina asked as she leaned forward at the table.

Lorinda just shrugged. She was on the verge of bursting out crying. That was the reason why she came to the coffee-house, because she didn't want to start bawling in front of her roommate, let alone her own son. A simple question like asking how she was doing just brought everything up.

"Oh, so I guess you're not talking to me," Regina said. "I see how you are. Of course, I didn't think that you of all people would shut me down like this, but I guess it's true that you really never know somebody. Have a nice life."

Lorinda, to her own surprise, started to rapidly shake her head as Regina pushed away from the table. "No, I'm happy to see you. It's just that −" and then she started to shake her head again. "I, I'm going through something right now."

Regina sat back down, as if she suddenly realized she misread the situation completely.

She reached her hand over to Lorinda's hand, and covered it. "I'm sorry. I guess I can be a real bitch sometimes. So, what's going on?"

Lorinda shook her head but then she told Regina the story of her son. "Frankie, you remember him, don't you?"

"Of course, your kid. Good kid. Why, what's going on with him?"

Lorinda took a deep breath. "He's sick. He's very sick. He has this kind of cancer, it's very rare in adults. And with kids, there's only been like 100 kids who have ever had this particular kind of cancer. It's mesothelioma, and −"

Regina narrowed her eyes. "Mesothelioma? That's caused by asbestos. By being exposed to asbestos for years and years."

Regina was now very interested in what Lorinda had to say.

Lorinda just nodded. "That's what the doctor says. But I don't know where he would've been exposed to asbestos, and I really don't know how he could have been exposed to as much as he needed to be exposed to in order to get it like this at his age. He's only seven years old. I really don't know how much longer he has. He's my entire life. I mean, my whole life. Everything I do, it's for him. Everything. I don't know how I'm going to have a reason for living after he goes. So, I guess I have to apologize to you for not reaching out more often. Truth be told, I really think I want to join him after he dies."

"Wait. There has to be something you can do for him."

"He's been doing chemo and radiation. I can't afford to get him into some of the experimental treatments that are not offering clinical trials. I've done the research. I know what's out there. I can't get my insurance company to pay for hardly anything. I mean, they pay for chemotherapy and radiation, things like that, but nothing's working for him, and I really want to get him into some of the other treatment options that I found. But I can't. So –"

"Okay. Here's the thing," Regina interrupted. "You have no idea how Frankie got sick, right?"

Lorinda nodded her head. "I mean, he must've been exposed to asbestos somehow."

"You ever use talcum powder on the kid?"

"Actually, no. I've known for a long time that talcum powder is bad. I've heard that for years. I don't use it, and I've never used it on Frankie."

"Have you talked to your landlord? Maybe your apartment has asbestos."

"Yes, that's the first thing I did. And inspectors said they could find no asbestos in my apartment or in my apartment building. I have a readout. I don't understand all of it, but the bottom line is that apparently my apartment and apartment building is clear of asbestos. I also reported my kid's disease to his school, and they opened up an investigation as well, and his school does not have any asbestos either. I suppose it's entirely possible that they're lying, or somebody's lying, I don't know. I just know that I don't have the emotional energy to fight these people. Especially because I don't really know where he got exposed to asbestos. All I know is that he has been."

"Well, we have to figure that out. If we can figure out what happened, how Frankie was exposed, I'm sure we can probably help your doctor in treating him. What kind of experimental therapies are out there now?"

"Immunotherapy. I guess that doctors can use a person's immunity system to fight the cancer. Also gene therapy. I don't really understand too much about that, except for I guess that the person's DNA gets mutated, so doctors can inject new DNA into cells. And there's another one, I don't really understand that one at all. I guess it's kinda like the gene therapy, but just a little bit different. I don't really know, because my insurance company won't cover any of it. So I just have to go with what they know about, and it's killing him. It's literally killing him, faster than the cancer is. Sometimes I think I should just stop. I mean, I don't want to put him through futile torment. I don't want his last days on earth to be miserable."

"Listen, I know you probably don't want to hear this, but you need to fight," Regina said. "Especially because you told me your kid is your life. I'm working for an attorney, Avery, she usually takes criminal cases, but she's a very good trial attorney. Why don't you let her talk to you? I mean, here's the thing. Number one, you need somebody to fight for you against your insurance company. It's bullshit that they're denying your right to try everything you can to get him well. I don't know a whole lot about the experimental therapies they're using for this particular disease, but I do know one thing. Any insurance company that will pay for just radiation and chemotherapy, and not even allow you to try something promising, that's just bullshit. I mean, just because you aren't wealthy, that means that you can't try gene therapy, or immunotherapy, or something like that? I'm going to have to have Avery take a look at your insurance policy and have her try to get the insurance company to get your kid covered. Believe me, insurance companies want you to give up. They want you just to not argue with them when they say they're not going to cover this or that. If you just go along with it, they win. And here you are, paying out the nose to them, and they're just going to not let you try everything you can?"

"I don't know what I can do. I mean, they said it's not covered, and that's what they say."

"Trust me on this, you get a lawyer involved with it, and they're suddenly going to play ball. I've seen that time and time again. But I think you also need to hire a lawyer because you need to figure out how your kid came in contact with asbestos in the first place. And then you need to sue the pants off of whoever poisoned your kid. You can't just take this lying down. This is your kid. It's your life. I know you don't have a lot of money, and that's fine. Avery will take the case, even if you don't have a dime. She'll take it on contingency. Do you know what that means?"

Lorinda fidgeted while she ate the salad that had just arrived at the table. She did kind of know what contingency meant, but not really. It was something about the lawyer not getting paid unless she wins, or something like that. But she was embarrassed to admit that she didn't really know what that term meant. "Yes, I know what it means."

"Okay, then. Listen, I know Avery has an opening tomorrow at three. Why don't you come to her office and she can set you up? She'll go through everything Frankie has been exposed to, and she'll try to figure out exactly what happened. And then she'll sue the crap out of the company that poisoned your kid."

"I can't do that. I have to work. I work every day from nine until three thirty."

"What are you doing these days?" Regina asked.

"Oh, this and that." Lorinda scratched her cheek, her eyes not meeting Regina's. "So, listen, I have to work, or I don't get paid. And if I don't get paid, Frankie's never going to have what he needs. He's never going to be able to die with any dignity. I really want to get him into hospice, but I can't afford that either. So all I can really do is watch him fade away, day by day, hour by hour, minute by minute. That's all I can do."

Grab your copy…
vinci-books.com/the-trial

About the Author

Rachel Sinclair was a criminal defense attorney for eleven years, so she doesn't scare easily. She graduated from the University of Missouri-Kansas City School of Law in 1998, and worked for the Public Defender's Office for several years before striking out on her own. She currently lives in San Diego, California, with her boyfriend, Joey, and her two fur babies, Annie and Toby. In her spare time, she likes to read, bicycle all over town, Boogie Board at the beach, and watch trashy television.